从雪豹到马雅可夫斯基

（汉英对照）

吉狄马加 ◎ 著

梅丹理、黄少政 ◎ 译

FROM
THE
LEOPARD
TO
MAYAKOVSKY

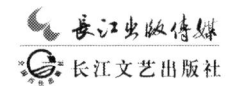

长江出版传媒
长江文艺出版社

吉狄马加

中国当代著名少数民族代表性诗人，同时也是一位具有广泛影响的国际性诗人，其诗歌已被翻译成二十多种文字，在近三十个国家或地区出版发行。曾获中国第三届诗歌奖、郭沫若文学奖荣誉奖、庄重文文学奖、肖洛霍夫文学纪念奖、柔刚诗歌成就奖、国际华人诗人笔会"中国诗魂奖"、南非姆基瓦人道主义奖、2016 欧洲诗歌与艺术荷马奖。2007 年创办青海湖国际诗歌节、青海国际诗人帐篷圆桌会议以及凉山西昌邛海国际诗歌周，现任中国作家协会副主席、书记处书记。

Jidi Majia is a representative figure among minority poets in China while also having broad influence as an international poet. His poetry has been translated into over 20 languages and published for distribution in 30 countries. He has been honored with Chinese literary awards including the Third China Poetry Prize, Guo Moruo Literature Prize, Zhuang Zhongwen Literary Prize, Shokhalov Memorial Prize, and Rougang Literary Prize. Outside of China he has won the Mkhiva International Humanitarian Award, the "China Poetic Spirit Award" of International Chinese P. E. N., and the 2016 European Poetry and Art Homer Award. Since 2007 he has founded three major serial poetry events: Qinghai International Poetry Festival; Qinghai Poets Tent Forum; and Xichang Qionghai Lake Poets Week. He currently serves as Deputy Chairman and Secretary- General of the Chinese Writers Association.

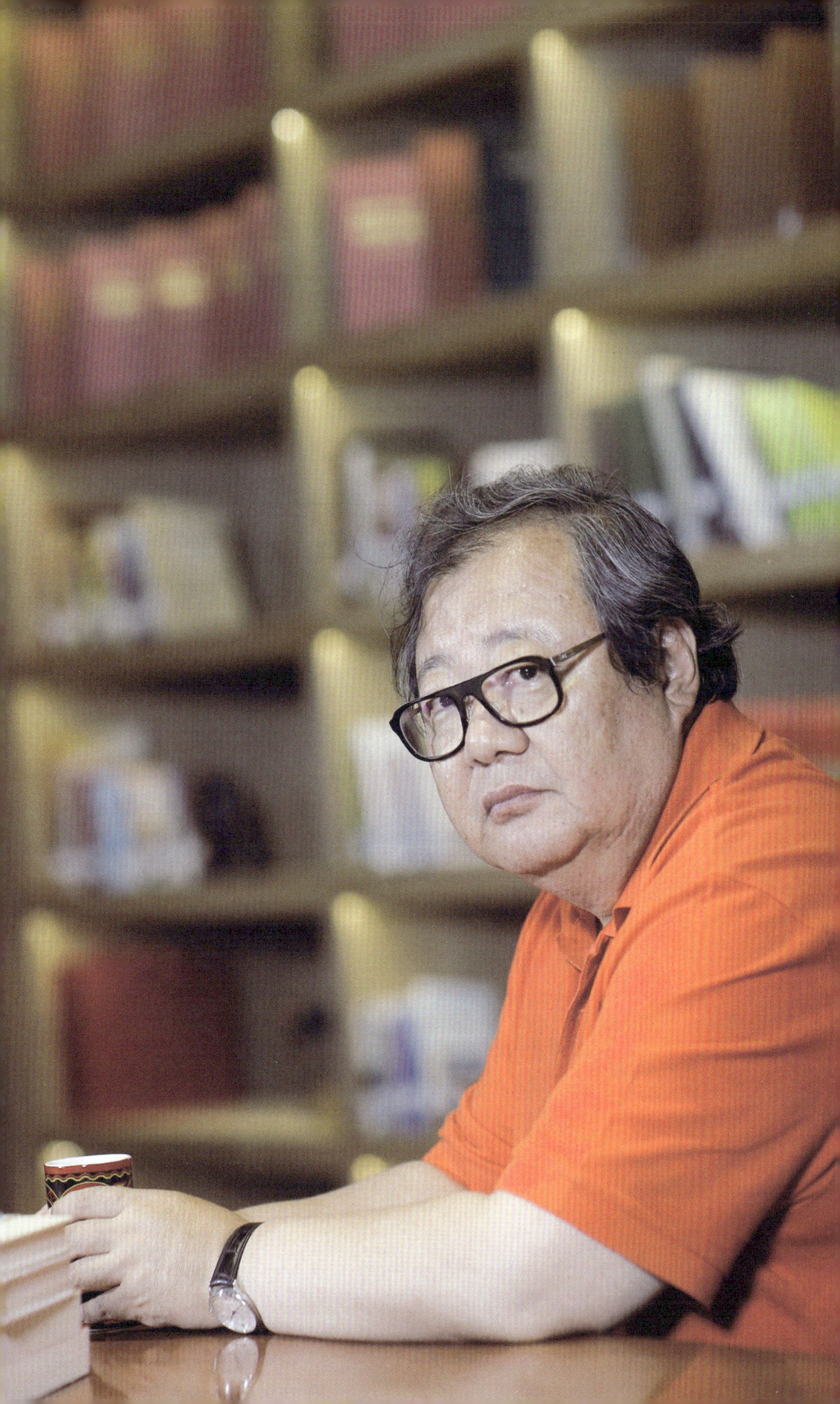

目　录

上　篇

2　圣地和乐土

8　我们的父亲——献给纳尔逊·曼德拉

14　无题——致诺尔德

16　雪的反光和天堂的颜色

24　致祖国

30　尼沙

34　口弦

38　河流

42　移动的棋子

46　而我——又怎能不回到这里！

50　耶路撒冷的鸽子

52　寻找费德里科·加西亚·洛尔加

56　致尤若夫·阿蒂拉

60　重新诞生的莱茵河——致摄影家安德烈斯·古斯基

64　如果我死了……

66　巨石上的痕迹——致 W. J. H. 铜像

3   Sacred Precinct, Blessed Ground

9   Our Father—Dedicated to Nelson Mandela

15 Untitled—For Nuoerde

17 Sunlit Snow and the Color of Heaven

25 To The Motherland

31 Mudd

35 Mouth Harp

39 River

43 The Moving Chess Piece

47 How Could I Not Want to Return Here!

51 A Dove of Jerusalem

53 In Search of Fredrico García Lorca

57 For Attila József

61 The Rhine River Reborn—To the photographer Andreas Gursky

65 If I Should Die…

67 Marks on a Megalith—for a bronze sculpture of W. J. H.

70　拉姆措湖的反光

72　致酒

76　我接受这样的指令

78　契约

80　鹰的葬礼

82　盲人

84　铜像

86　流亡者——写给诗人阿多尼斯和他流离失所的人民

90　黑色——写给马列维奇和我们自己

92　金骏马

96　刺穿的心脏——写给吉茨安·尤斯金诺维奇·塔比泽

100　诗人的结局

106　致叶夫图申科

108　没有告诉我

110　谁也不能高过你的头颅——献给屈原

116　我，雪豹……——献给乔治·夏勒

150　致马雅可夫斯基

182　不朽者

71   The Shimmers of Lamutso Lake

73   To Wine

77   A Command Accepted

79   Contract

81   The Eagle's Funeral

83   The Blind Man

85   Bronze Bust

87   THE EXILE—For the poet Adonis and his uprooted countrymen

91   Blackness—For Malevich and for ourselves

93   Golden Steed

97   Your Pierced Heart—For Titsian Tabidze

101 The Outcome of a Poet

107 For Yevtushenko

109 Not Told

111 No One Can Overshadow Your Skull—Dedicated to Qu Yuan

117 I, Snow Leopard…—Dedicated to George Schaller

151 For Vladimir Mayakovsky

183 The Enduring One

下 篇

236 "柔刚诗歌奖"颁奖会上的致答辞
242 在为费尔南多·伦东·梅里诺颁发青海湖国际诗歌节国际诗歌交流贡献奖会上的致辞
246 青海湖国际诗歌节宣言
250 山地族群的生存记忆与被拯救中的边缘影像
　　——在2014中国（青海）世界山地纪录片节圆桌会议上的发言
258 向诗歌致敬——在2014国际诗人帐篷圆桌会议上的致辞
262 诗歌的本土写作和边缘的声音
　　——在2014青海国际诗人帐篷圆桌会议上的演讲
270 诗歌是人类迈向明天最乐观的理由
　　——在2015青海湖国际诗歌节开幕式上的致辞
276 何为诗人？何为诗？
　　——2016西昌邛海"丝绸之路"国际诗歌周开幕式演讲
282 一个中国诗人的非洲情结
　　——在2014南非姆基瓦人道主义大奖颁奖仪式上的书面致答辞
294 在2016欧洲诗歌与艺术荷马奖颁奖仪式上的致辞

237   Reply to the 20 Rougang Poetry Award Ceremony

243   Address to Fernando Rendon by Jidi Majia at the Ceremony of Presenting an Award in Honor of Fernando Rendon's Outstanding Contribution to Promote World Poetry Movement

247   Manifesto of Qinghai Lake International Poetry

251   Existential Memory of Mountain Inhabitants and Marginalized Images Coming to the Rescue
      Key - note Address at the 2014 Roundtable Forum of Qinghai World Mountain Documentary Festival

259   A Tribute to Poetry
      A Speech Given at the Poetic Evening Dedicated to Humanity of the Tent Roundtable Forum of World Poets

263   Localized Poetic Writing and marginalized Voice
      Key - note Speech Delivered at the Opening Ceremony of 2014 Tent Roundtable Forum of World Poets

271   Why Poetry Still Matters Today?
      A Speech given by Jidi Majia, chairman of Qinghai Lake Intl Poetry Festival, deputy chairman of All China Writers Union

277   Who Is a Poet? What Is Poetry?
      Jidi Majia   deputy chairman of All China Writers Association Address at the Opening Ceremony of Xichang. Qionghai 2016 Silk Road Intl Poetry Week

283   The African Complex of A Chinese Poet
      Written Speech at 2014 Mkiva Humanitarian Award Ceremony

295   Noble Literature Is Still of Interest and Moment
      Acceptance Speech at the Awarding Ceremony of The European Medal of Poetry and Art Homer 2016

298   THE EUROPEAN MEDAL OF POETRY AND ART

上篇

圣地和乐土

在那里。在那青海湖的东边,
风一遍遍,吹过了
被四季装点的节日。
尽管我找不到鸟儿飞行的方向,
我却能从不同的地方,
远远地眺望到
那些星罗棋布的庄廓。
并且我还能看见,两只雪白的鸽子,
如同一对情侣般的天使,
一次又一次消失在时间的深处!
在那里——天空是最初的创造,
布满了彩陶云霓一样的纹路,
以及踩高跷人的影子,这样的庆典,
已经成为千年的仪式!
谁是这里的主人?野牦牛喉管里
喷射的鲜血,见证了公正无私的太阳,
是如何照亮了这片土地。
在那里。星月升起的时间已经很久,
传说净化成透明的物体。
这是人类在高处选择的
圣地和乐土。在这里——
河流的光影上涌动着不朽者

Sacred Precinct, Blessed Ground

There, on the east side of Qinghai Lake

Wind blows and blows, past festivals

That take the four seasons for adornment.

I cannot make out where birds are flying,

Yet from different vantage points,

I can gaze upon hamlets laid out

Like constellations on a chessboard.

I also see two snow-white doves,

Like a pair of infatuated angels,

Time and again receding in time's depths.

In that place, empty sky is the original creation,

Streaked with cirrus markings like painted pottery;

Up close are shapes of stilt-walkers; this festive display

Has become a thousand-year ritual.

Who are the masters here? Blood pulsing in the neck

Of a wild yak testifies to the sun's impartial way

Of shining on this piece of ground.

There, moon and stars have been rising so long,

Legends say they cleansed themselves into crystalline orbs.

This is the sacred precinct, the blissful ground

Mankind has chosen. In this place—

Eddies of a dappled river write names of the undying

轮回的名字。这里不是宿命的开始，
而是一曲光明和诞生的颂歌。
无数的部族居住在这里，
把生和死雕刻成了神话。
在那里。在高原与高原的过渡地带，
为了生命的延续，颂辞穿越了
虚无的城池，最终抵达了
生殖力最强的流域。在那里——
小麦的清香从远处传来，温暖的
灶坑里烘烤着金黄的土豆。
在那里——花儿与少年，从生唱到死，
从死唱到生，它是这个世界
最为动人心魄的声音！
不知有多少爱情的故事，
在他们的对唱中，潜入了
万物的灵魂和骨髓。在那里——
或许也曾有过小小的纷争，
但对于千百年来的和睦共处，
它们又是多么的微乎其微。
是伟大的传统和历史的恩赐，给与了
这里的人民无穷无尽的生存智慧！
在那里——在那青海湖的东边，
在那一片高原谷地，或许这一切，
总有一天都会成为一种记忆。
但是这一切，又绝不仅仅是这些。
因为在这个星球上，直到今天
人类间的杀戮并没有消失和停止。

Who reincarnate here. This is not the start of a fixed fate,
But a paean to being born in the light.
Countless tribes dwell here,
Carving birth and death into mythology.
Here, on the plateau and its transition zone,
For life to go on, praise songs must pass over
The moat of nothingness, at last arriving
In the watershed of full fertility. In that place—
Scent of wheat wafts from afar, and warmth spreads
From amber potatoes roasting in a fire pit.
There, youths and flowers sing from birth to death,
Then from death to birth, and their song
Is most stirring of all the world's sounds!
Who knows how many love stories,
Carried in their songs, slipped into
The soul and marrow of all things! In that place—
There may have been times of minor strife,
But all that is negligible when measured
Against centuries of sharing the land in peace.
Honored tradition and bountiful history gave them
Reserves of wisdom about how one should live.
In that place, on the east side of Qinghai Lake,
In a basin on the plateau, all that is found there
May someday be no more than a memory.
Yet what is found there is surely more than this,
Because on this planet, up until today
Slaughter of men by men has not gone away.

在那里——在那青海湖的东边!

人类啊!这是比黄金更宝贵的启示,

它让我们明白了一个真理——

那就是永久的和平和安宁,只能来自于

包容、平等、共生、互助和对生命的尊重!

而不会再有其他!

In that place—on the east side of Qinghai Lake,

Humanity, there is a lesson here more precious than gold,

It makes the truth clear to us—

That eternal peace and calm can only come

From tolerance and equality, from sharing space and food, and from honoring life!

There can be no other way!

我们的父亲
——献给纳尔逊·曼德拉

我仰着头——想念他!
只能长久地望着无尽的夜空
我为那永恒的黑色再没有回声
而感到隐隐的不安,风已经停止了吹拂
只有大海的呼吸,在远方的云层中
闪烁着悲戚的光芒
是在一个片刻,还是在某一个瞬间
在我们不经意的时候
他已经站在通往天堂的路口
似乎刚刚转过身,在向我们招手
脸上露出微笑,这是属于他的微笑
他的身影开始渐渐地远去
其实,我们每一个人都知道
他要去的那个地方,就是灵魂的安息之地
那个叫库努的村落,正准备迎接他的回归
纳尔逊·曼德拉——我们的父亲
当他最初离开这里的时候,在那金色的阳光下
一个黑色的孩子,开始了漫长的奔跑
那个孩子不是别人——那是他昨天的影子
一双明亮的眼睛,注视着无法预知的未来
那是他童年的时光被记忆分割成的碎片
他的双脚赤裸着,天空中的太阳

Our Father
—Dedicated to Nelson Mandela

I raise my head—missing him!
Yet can only gaze at the endless night sky
The lack of an echo from that eternal blackness
Makes unease steal over me; not a gust of wind stirs
Only the breath of sea is heard, through far clouds
That is flickering with mournful light
Perhaps in a short interval, a fleeting instant
When I was hardly paying attention
His feet were placed on that crossing bound for Heaven
He seems to have turned about, his arm is waving at us
A smile shows on his face, a smile that is his alone
His figure begins to recede into the distance
In fact, as each of us knows in our own way
He has headed toward the resting place of souls
Now Qunu village prepares to receive the returnee
Nelson Mandela—our father
When he first left that place, a black child
Under golden sunlight, to begin his long, hurried journey
That very child and no other, prefigured the man to come
A pair of shining eyes, a level gaze at the unknown future
A childhood cut short, to be retrieved in fragments of memory
Hours of going barefoot and a moment under the sky

在他的头顶最终成为一道光束

只有宇宙中坠落的星星，才会停留在

黑色部族歌谣的最高潮

只有那永不衰竭的舞蹈的节奏

能够遗忘白色，找到消失的自信

为了祖先的祭品，被千百次地赞颂

所有的渴望，只有在被夜色

全部覆盖的时候，才会穿越生和死

从这里出发，就是一种宿命

他将从此把自己的生命——与数以千万计的

黑色大众的生命联系在一起

他将不再为自己而活着，并时刻准备着

为一个种族的解放而献身

从这里出发，只能做如下的选择

选择死——因为生早已成为偶然

选择别离——因为相聚已成为过去

选择流亡——因为追逐才刚刚开始

选择高墙——因为梦中才会出现飞鸟

选择呐喊——因为沉默在街头被警察杀死

选择镣铐——因为这样更多的手臂才能自由

选择囚禁——因为能让无数的人享受新鲜的空气

为了这样一个选择，他只能义无反顾

因为他的选择，用去的时间——

不会是一天，也不会是一年，而将是漫长的岁月

就是他本人也根本不会知道

他梦想的这一天将会何时真的到来

谁会知道？一个酋长的儿子

将从这里选择一条道路，从那一天开始

When a ray of sunlight and the crown of his head became one

From vast space a star was bound to fall, and its visit

Chanced to come at the high point of a chanted song

Only because that dance's rhythm never faltered

Could whiteness be forgotten and confidence regained

So offerings to forefathers could send up renewed praise

All wishes had to be enclosed in night's blackness

Before they could pass beyond life and death

His setting forth from here was ordained by fate

Henceforth he would bind his own life

To millions of lives among the black crowd

He did not live for himself, was always ready

For the self- sacrifice that would liberate a race

Setting forth from here, he had to make choices

To choose death—because survival was just a random chance

To choose parting—because togetherness belonged to the past

To choose exile—because the hounding was far from over

To choose brick walls—because a bird could fly only in dreams

To choose outcry—because silence was slaughtered in the streets

To choose handcuffs—because other arms needed to be set free

To choose captivity—for countless others who needed a breath of air

To embrace such a choice meant there was no turning back

This choice he had to make would demand his time

Not one day or year, but a long stretch of seasons

He did not have the slightest way of knowing

When the day he dreamed of would really come

Who could have known? That this tribal leader's son

Would choose such a road, from that place, starting that day

就是这样一个人，已经注定改变了二十世纪的历史
是的，从这里出发，尽管这条路上
陪伴他的将是监禁、酷刑、迫害以及随时的死亡
但是他从未放弃，当他从那——
牢狱的窗户外听见大海的涛声
他曾为人类为追求自由和平等的梦想而哭泣
谁会知道，一个有着羊毛一样鬈发的黑孩子
曾经从这里出发，然而他始终只有一个目标
那就是带领大家，去打开那一扇——
名字叫自由的沉重的大门！
为了这个目标，他九死一生从未改变
谁会知道，就是这个黑色民族的骄子
不，他当然绝不仅仅属于一个种族
是他让我们明白了一个真理，那就是爱和宽恕
能将一切仇恨的坚冰融化
而这一切，只有他，因为他曾经被另一个
自认为优越的种族国家长时间地监禁
而他的民族更是被奴役和被压迫的奴隶
只有他，才有这样的资格——
用平静而温暖的语言告诉人类
——"忘记仇恨"！
我仰着头——泪水已经模糊了双眼
我长时间注视的方向，在地球的另一边
我知道——我们的父亲——他就要入土了
他将被永远地安葬在那个名字叫库努的村落
我相信，因为他——从此以后
人们会从这个地球的四面八方来到这里
而这个村落也将会因此成为人类良心的圣地！

That he was the one, born to change 20th-century history
Yes, he set forth on that road, and what kept him company
Was prison time, torture, persecution and imminent death
But he never gave up; he always listened for
Sounds of ocean surf from outside his prison window
Wept for dreams of freedom and equality that he sought for mankind
Who would have known? A black child growing a fleece of curly hair
Would depart from such a place, keeping a single goal in mind
Which was to rally everyone behind him
And help them open the heavy door of freedom
Of nine lives he lost all but one, never swerving from his goal
Who would have known, that this favored son of the black race
Who of course cannot be claimed by one race alone
Would help us understand the truth of love and forgiveness
That nothing else could melt the icy mass of hatred?
It could only have been him, to have been jailed so long
Watching his people conscripted and treated as slaves
By a racial state that assumed its own superiority
It could only have been him, qualified in such a way
That he could tell mankind in his quiet, gentle voice
— "Forget about hatred!"
I raise my head—by now my eyes swim with tears
Where I direct my gaze, on the other side of the globe
I know that he—our father—will soon be lowered into earth
He will rest in peace forever under the soil of Qunu village
He gives me good reason to believe—from now on
People from all corners of the earth will visit that village
It will thus become a sacred site of human conscience!

无　题

　　——致诺尔德

我们都拥有过童年的时光

那时候，你的梦曾被巍峨的雪山滋养

同样是在幻想的年龄，宽广的草原

从一开始就教会了你善良和谦恭

当然更是先辈们的传授，你才找到了

打开智慧之门的钥匙

常常有这样的经历，一个人呆望着天空

而心灵却充盈着无限的自由

诺尔德，但今天当我们回忆起

慈母摇篮边充满着爱意的歌谣

生命就如同那燃烧的灯盏，转瞬即逝

有时候它更像太阳下的影子，不等落日来临

就已经消失得无影无踪

亲爱的朋友，我们都是文字的信徒

请相信人生不过是一场短暂的戏剧

唯有精神和信仰创造的世界

才能让我们的生命获得不朽的价值！

Untitled

—For Nuoerde

We have all possessed childhood hours, and in that time
Your dreams were nourished by lofty snow- capped peaks
Likewise at an age prone to fantasy, the wide grassland
Right from the start taught you kindness and humility
Of course the lore passed down by elders helped more
To find the key that would open wisdom's door
At times one would be found alone, gazing at the sky
And one's heart would be filled with boundless freedom
Nuoerde, as we summon up memories today
Of kind mothers and their loving cradle- side songs
Life like a burning lamp passes quickly
Sometimes like a shadow at sundown
Disappearing with no trace, before the sun even sets
Dear friend, we are both believers in the written word
Please believe that life is a brief stage show
Only the world created by spirit and faith
Can confer undying value upon our lives!

雪的反光和天堂的颜色

1

这是门的孕育过程
是古老的时间,被水净洗的痕迹
这是门——这是门!
然而永远看不见
那隐藏在背后的金属的叹息
这是被火焰铸造的面具
它在太阳的照耀下
弥漫着金黄的倦意
这是门——这是门!
它的质感就如同黄色的土地
假如谁伸手去抚摸
在这高原永恒的寂静中
没有啜泣,只有长久地沉默……

2

那是神鹰的眼睛
不,或许只有上帝
才能从高处看见,这金色的原野上
无数的生命被抽象后

Sunlit Snow and the Color of Heaven

1

A door is being gestated here, in this place of ageless time
Bearing signatures of cleansing by water
A door is here—a door!
Yet it is forever unseen
That sigh of concealed metal ore
Is behind a mask forged by intense fire
Under the sun's radiance
Pervaded by golden languor
A door is here—a door!
Its texture is akin to yellow earth
For someone whose hand reaches caressingly
Amid this plateau's eternal stillness
There are no sobs, only stretches of silence…

2

It would take the divine eagle's eye
Or perhaps none other than God on High
Could see the dappled markings
Made by countless beings of the highland
As they are abstracted under gold- hued light

所形成的斑斓的符号
遥远的迁徙已经停止
牛犊在倾听小草的歌唱
一只蚂蚁缓慢地移动
牵引着一丝来自天宇的光

3

蓝色,蓝色,还是蓝色
在这无名的乡间
这是被反复覆盖的颜色
这是蓝色的血液,没有限止地流淌
最终凝固成的生命的意志
这是纯粹的蓝宝石,被冰冷的燃烧熔化
这是蓝色的睡眠——
在深不可测的潜意识里
看见的最真实的风暴!

4

风吹拂着——
在这苍秋的高空
无疑这风是从遥远的地方吹来的
只有在风吹拂着的时候
而时间正悄然滑过这样的季节
当大雁从村庄的头顶上飞过
留下一段不尽的哀鸣
此时或许才会有人目睹

A far- ranging migration has come to rest

A young calf pauses to hear grass- blades singing

A single ant traverses a patch of earth

Tugging a thread of light from the sky's vault

3

Blue, blue, and still more blue

In this nameless precinct

Color is painted repeatedly over color

Here is blood of blue color, trickling endlessly

At last coalescing in the will to live

Purest lapis lazuli, melted by fire now iced over

This is blue- hued slumber—

Most genuine tempest to be found

In unplumbed depths of subconscious mind

4

Wind blows caressingly

Under the high skies of sere autumn

Surely it first stirred in some remote places

And even now as it brushes by

The season's hours slip away

As a flock of geese fly over a village

Trailing its continual broken cries

At such times a prayer flag may bear witness

在那经幡的一面——生命开始诞生
而在另一面——死亡的影子已经降临!

5

你的雪山之巅
仅仅是一个象征,它并非是现实的存在
因为现实中的雪山,它的冰川
已经开始不可逆转地消失
谁能忍心为雪山致一篇悼辞?
为何很少听见人类的忏悔?
雪山之巅,反射出幽暗的光芒
它永远在记忆和梦的边缘浮现
但愿你的创造是永恒的
因为你用一支抽象的画笔
揭示并记录了一个悲伤的故事!

6

那是疯狂的芍药
跳荡在大地生殖力最强的部位
那是云彩的倒影,把水的词语
抒写在紫色的疆域
穿越沙漠的城市,等待河流的消息
没有选择,闪光的秋叶
摇动着羚羊奔跑的箭矢
疾风中的牦牛,冰川时期的化石
只有紧紧地握住手中的法器
占卜的神枝才会敲响预言的皮鼓

From this side—to life being born
From that—to the descent of death's shadow!

5

For us the snow- covered mountain peaks
Remain more in the mind's eye than in reality
Because peaks had glaciers, but in reality
They are showing signs of irreversible loss
Who can bear to offer elegies for snowy peaks?
Why is human repentance so seldom heard?
Reflected light from snowy peaks grows dim
Always looming at the edge of dream and memory
If only your creative works could endure
You who wield an abstract paintbrush
So this tragic story may be revealed and recorded

6

What an exuberant bed of peonies
Hopscotches out of the earth's most fertile layer
Showing inverted shapes of clouds, and the logos of water
Is inscribed in that violet- hued region!
Having passed through urban gulches, ready for a river's message
Given no choice, a quaking autumn leaf catches light
An antelope's bounding arrow is set in motion
Here are yaks facing a gale, fossils of a glacial age
Only if sacred implements are taken in hand firmly
Can a diviner's stick beat the drum of prophecy

7

你告诉我高原的夜空
假如长时间地去注视
就会发现，肉体和思想开始分离
所有的群山、树木、岩石都白银般剔透
高空的颜色，变幻莫测，隐含着暗示
有时会听见一阵遥远的雷声
我们都不知道什么是最后的审判
但是，当我们仰望着这样的夜空
我们会相信——
创造这个世界的力量确实存在
而最后的审判已经开始……

8

谁看见过天堂的颜色？
这就是我看见的天堂的颜色，你肯定地说！
首先我相信天堂是会有颜色的
而这种颜色一定是温暖的
我相信这种颜色曾被人在生命中感受过
我还相信这种颜色曾被我们呼吸
毫无疑问，它是我们灵魂中的另一个部分
因为你，我开始想象天堂的颜色
就如同一个善于幻想的孩子
我常常闭着眼睛，充满着感激和幸福
有时泪水也会不知不觉地夺眶而出……

7

You speak of the night sky over this plateau
After a long spell of star- gazing you find
Flesh and thought begin to part company
Each peak, tree and boulder looks like new- minted silver
The sky's color is unfathomable, holding portents
Distant thunder is heard from time to time
None of us know what the final judgment will be
But if only we gaze awhile at this night sky
Belief in the power that creates this world
And the reckoning that has already begun
Will surely be brought home to us...

8

Who has seen the color of heaven?
I have seen it here, you proclaim!
First of all I am sure that heaven has a color
And that this color does not lack warmth
I believe this color was felt in others' lives
I even believe we have inhaled this color
Without a doubt, it is one portion of our souls
Because of you, I begin to imagine heaven's color
Like a child prone to fantasies
I often close my eyes, filled with gratitude and blessings
Sometimes tears in my eyes brim and overflow

致祖国

我的祖国
是东方的一棵巨人树
那黄色的土地上,永不停息地
流淌着的是一条条金色的河流
我的祖国
那纯粹的蓝色
是天空和海洋的颜色
那是一只鸟,双翅上
闪动着黄金的雨滴
正在穿越黎明的拂晓

我的祖国,在神话中成长
那青铜的树叶
发出过千百次动人的声响
我的祖国,从来
就不属于一个民族
因为她有五十六个儿女
而我的民族,那五十六分之一
却永远属于我的祖国

我的祖国的历史
不应该被随意割断

To The Motherland

My Motherland

Is a broad- limbed giant of the Orient

Over yellow earth run ceaseless currents

Of her many golden rivers

My Motherland

Has pure blueness

In the color of sky and ocean

It is a bird with golden droplets

Glinting on its wings

As it passes through dawn's early light

Motherland, while you were growing up in myths

From that bronze- leaved tree

Was heard a thousand thrilling noises

My Motherland never belonged

To any single ethnic group

Because her children number fifty- six

And my ethnic group, which is one fifty- sixth

Forever belongs to my Motherland

This history of my Motherland

Should not be willfully cut apart

无论她承载的是

光辉的年轮，还是屈辱的生活

因为我的祖国的历史

是一本完整的历史

当我们赞颂唐朝的时候

又怎能遗忘元朝开辟过的疆域

当我们梦回宋词的国度

在那里寻找文字的力量

又怎能真的去轻视

大清开创的伟业，不凡的气度

我说我的祖国的历史，是一部

完整的历史，那是因为我把这一切

都看成是我的祖国

血肉之躯不可分割的部分

我的祖国，我想对你说

当有一天你需要并选择我们

你的选择，一定不是简单的

由于地域的因素，不同的背景

不仅仅是因为我们来自哪一个民族

同样也不要因为我们的族别

而让我们，失去了真正平等竞争的机会

我的祖国，我希望我们对你的

一万个忠诚，最终换来的

是你对我们的百分之百的信任

Whatever chapters it includes

Brilliant or shameful as they may be

Because my Motherland's history

Is a story which has its own completeness

When moved to praise the Tang dynasty

Let us not forget the Mongols' far-flung frontiers

When going back in dreams to the lyric-loving Song

Searching for what lent force to their written words

It would hardly be right to overlook

The attainments and elan of the Qing dynasty

When I speak of the Motherland's history

I see it whole, because everything those eras were

Were a part of my Motherland's corporeal body

That is never to be dismembered

My Motherland, I wish to say to you

When the day comes you need to choose us

Your choice will surely not be simple

There are regional considerations, matters of background

Not just because we come from a certain ethnic group

Likewise do not make our ethnicity the reason

For depriving us of chances to compete equally

My Motherland, I hope that our loyalty to you

Shown in countless ways, will ultimately win us

One hundred percent of your trust

我的祖国

那优美的合唱，已经被证明

是五十六个民族语言的总和

离开其中任何一位歌手的参与

那壮丽的和声都不完美

就如同我的民族的声音

或许它来自遥远的边缘

但是它的存在

却永远不可或缺

就如同我们彝人古老的文字

它所记载的全部所有的一切

毫无疑问，都已成为

你那一部辉煌巨著中的

足以让人自豪的不朽的篇章

我的祖国，请原谅

我的大胆和诗人才会有的真实

我希望你看中我们的是，而只能是

作为一个人所具有的高尚的品质

卓越的能力，真正摒弃了自私和狭隘

以及那无与伦比的，蕴含在

个体生命之中的，最为宝贵的

能为这个国家和大众去服务的牺牲精神

我的祖国，我希望并热忱地期待着

你看中我们的是，当然也只能是

我们对你的忠诚，就像

血管里的每一滴鲜血

都来自于正在跳动的心脏

而永远不会是其他！

My Motherland
The beauty of your chorus
Has been proven to be a synthesis
Of languages spoken by your fifty-six peoples
If any of these singers could not join in
That grand harmony would be less than perfect
The voice of my ethnic group is one example
It may come from a remote borderland
Even so its existence
Is forever indispensable
Just as the ancient writing of the Yi people
And the sum of what that writing records
Is beyond doubt a chapter worthy of pride
In your illustrious compendium

My Motherland, please forgive
My boldness and my poet's frankness
I hope what you value in me is no less than
My sterling qualities as a human being, and that you
Find me highly able and free from narrow self-interest
And that my precious spirit of service to nation and people
Seated deep in the core of my being
Is not overshadowed by anyone
My Motherland, it is my hope and ardent expectation
That what you value in me is no less
Than my loyalty to you, just as
Every drop of blood in my veins
Pulses from one beating heart
For there can be no other!

尼 沙

尼沙，是一个人的名字？
或者说仅仅是一个词
没有任何实际的意义
要不就是一个真实的存在
是这个地球七十亿人口中的一分子
不知道，是不是更早的时候
你们曾漫步街头
你们曾穿越雨季
要不直到如今，你还怅然若失
还能回想起那似乎永远
遗失了的碎片般的踪迹
或许这一切仅仅是个假设
尼沙，注定将擦肩而过
当一列火车疾驰穿过站台
送行者的眼睛已被泪水迷蒙
再也听不到汽笛的鸣叫
这片刻更像置身于虚幻的场景
当然，这可能也是一个幻觉
尼沙，或许从未存在过
无论是作为一个人，还是
作为语言中一个不存在的词
它只是想象中的一种记忆

Mudd

Mudd, is this a person's name?

Or is it merely a word

Without any real meaning?

Or else it stands for a genuine entity

One of seven billion who populate the earth

I don't know if you ever trudged

Along the street in an earlier time

And had to go through rainy spells

Or if you are still there, dejected and bereft

Able to recollect the fragmentary trace

Of something that seems forever gone

Or maybe this is all just supposition

Mudd, fated to brush by unmet

As the accelerating train leaves a station

The sender- off's eyes are swimming in tears

Not hearing the steam whistle's blast

Placed for a moment in an alternate setting

Of course, this may only be a fantasy

Mudd, perhaps you have never existed

Whether as a person, or a word

Not really there in language

Just an imaginary memory

永远无法判定有多少真实的成分
因为隔着时空能听到的
只是久远的模糊的声音
我不知道，你是否真的
开始过无望的漫长的寻找
如果不是命运真的会再给你一次机会
可以肯定，你敲开的每一扇门
它只会通向永恒的虚无，在那里
有的只是消失在时间深处的影子
你不会找到半点你需要的东西
尼沙，是一个真实的存在还是幻想
我想，无需再去寻找更多的证据
因为从那双动人的眼睛里，是你
看见过沙漠黎明时的微光
闪耀着露水般晶莹的涟漪，你的
脸庞曾被另一个生命分泌的气味和物质
笼罩，那裙裾飘动着，有梦一样的暗花
你还记得，你匍匐在这温暖的沙漠上
畅饮过人世间最美最甜的甘泉
而这一切，对你而言已经足够

尼沙，是否真的存在并不重要……

Its proportion of realness is not easy to determine

For there is a temporal gap, and across it

Only vague, faraway voices can be heard

I do not know if you ever truly began

Your prolonged and hopeless search

Had fate not truly given you another chance

Whatever door you might have pushed open

Would have led to eternal blankness, and shadows

If there at all, would have faded into time's depths

Never yielding up the slightest thing you needed

Mudd…was that a real being or an illusion?

I think there is no need to search for evidence

Because there was a pair of stirring eyes

In which you saw dawn's glow over a desert

They flashed their dewy, pellucid ripples, and your face

Was surrounded by exudations from another living thing

In the sway of that skirt was a dreamlike hidden flower

You still recall yourself, stretched on warm desert sand

Gulping from the sweetest spring known to man

And for you now, all this is sufficient

Whether Mudd existed hardly matters

口　弦[①]

弹拨口弦的时候
黑暗笼罩着火塘。
伸手不见五指
只有口弦的声音。
口弦的弹奏
是一种隐秘的词汇
是被另一个听者
捕获的暗语。
它所表达的意义
永远不会，停留在
空白的地域。
它的弹拨
只有口腔的共鸣。
它的音量
细如游丝，
它是这个世界
最小的乐器。
一旦口弦响起来
在寂静的房里
它的倾诉，就会
占领所有的空间。
它不会选择等待

Mouth Harp[①]

When the mouth harp is played
Darkness envelops the fireplace.
Fingers before one's face are hard to see,
There is only the mouth harp's sound.
The plucking of the mouth harp
Holds a hidden vocabulary
A code that is grasped
By another person who listens.
The meaning it conveys
Will never come to a stop
In a zone of blankness.
The plucked strip only resonates
In the cavity of a mouth.
Its sound is fine in volume
Like floating floss.
In this world it is
The smallest musical instrument.
Once a mouth harp emits its sound
In a quiet room
Its confession will occupy
Every corner of that space.
It does not choose to wait

只会抵达，另一个

渴望中的心灵。

口弦从来不是

为所有的人弹奏。

但它微弱的诉说

将会在倾听者的灵魂里

掀起一场

看不见的风暴!

①口弦，彝族人的一种原始乐器，用竹片或铜片做成，演奏时用口腔共鸣，音质优美，声音微弱而细小。

It can only arrive—in a heart
Which also strains with longing
One does not play a mouth harp
For any and every person,
But in the hearts of those who listen
To its delicate plaint
It will surely stir up
An invisible storm!

①*The Yi mouth harp is a primitive musical instrument which produces resonant sounds by vibrating a strip of brass or bamboo held next to the mouth cavity.*

河　流

阿合诺依[①]——
你这深沉而黑色的河流
我们民族古老的语言
曾这样为你命名！

你从开始就有别于
这个世界其他的河流
你穿越我们永恒的故土
那高贵庄严的颜色
闪烁在流动着的水面

你流淌着
在我们传诵的史诗中
已经有数千年的历史
或许这个时间
还要更加久长

我们的祖先
曾在你的岸边憩息
是你那甘甜的乳汁
让他们遗忘了
漫长征途的艰辛，以及
徐徐来临的倦意

River

Ah- he- nuo- yi[①]—
You Black Deep River
In the ancient language of my people
This is how you are named

Right from the start you were different
From any other river in the world
You pass through our eternal native ground
With that noble, solemn color
Ever wavering on your fluid surface.

Your current has run
In the epics we recite
Down through millennia of history
And perhaps from this time on

You will run in ages to come

Along your banks our ancestors
Once found rest and replenishment
It was your sweet milk
That enabled them to forget
Weariness that stole over them
And the ordeals of their long expedition

他们的脸庞,也曾被
你幽深的灵魂照亮

你奔腾不息
在那茫茫的群山和峡谷
那仁慈宽厚的声音
就如同一支歌谣
把我们忧郁的心抚慰
在渐渐熄灭的火塘旁
当我们沉沉地睡去
潜入无边的黑暗
只有你会浮现在梦中
那黑色孕育的光芒
将把我们所有的
苦难和不幸的记忆
都全部地一扫而空

阿合诺依——我还知道
只要有彝人生活的地方
就不会有人,不知晓
你这父亲般的名字
我们的诗歌,赞颂过
无数的河流
然而,对你的赞颂
却比它们更多!

①阿合诺依,彝语的意思是黑色幽深的河流,这里指中国西南部的金沙江,是作者故乡的一条大河。

Your deeply grounded soul
Once lit up their countenances

You run headlong through chasms
Past mountains stretching out of sight
Your benign, expansive sound
Is like a folksong
Consoling our brooding hearts
Beside the fading embers of a fireplace
As we fall asleep
We slip into boundless blackness
You—most of all—appear in our dreams
And rays incubated within blackness
Will sweep away in an instant
All of our memories
Of bitterness and hardship

Ah- he- nuo- yi, I can be sure
In whatever place Yi people live
There is no one who does not know
The name of you—their father
Our poems have given praise
To countless rivers
Yet the greater portion of praise
Has always gone to you!

①*Ah−he−nuo−yi in the Yi language means "Black Deep River." Here it refers to the river which in Chinese is called Jinsha Jiang. It is a major river in the writer's homeland.*

移动的棋子

相信指头,其实更应该相信
手掌的不确定,因为它的木勺
并不只对自己,那手纹的反面
空白的终结,或许只在夜晚
相信手掌,但手臂的临时颠倒
却让它猝不及防,像一个侍者
相信手臂,可是身体别的部分
却发出了振聋发聩的呻吟,因为
手臂无法确定两个同样的时刻
相信身体,然而影子的四肢
并不具有揉碎灵魂的短斧
相信思想,弧形的一次虚构
让核心的躯体,抵达可怕的深渊
不对比的高度,钉牢了残缺的器官
相信自由的意志,在无限的时间
之外,未知的事物背信弃义
没有唯一,只有巨石上深刻的"3"
相信吹动的形态,在第四维
星群神秘的迁徙,只有多或少
黑暗的宇宙布满规律的文字
相信形而上的垂直,那白色的铁
可是谁能证实?在人类的头顶之上

The Moving Chess Piece

Trust the finger…in fact it would be better to trust
The indecision of the palm, because its ladle shape
Is not just for itself, and the complement to its palm print—
Putting an end to blankness—comes perhaps only at night
Trust the palm, but the arm gone akimbo is too quick
For the palm to cope with; the palm waits in attendance
Trust the arm, but another part of the body
Makes deafening moans, because the arm
Cannot decide between two similar moments
Trust the body, yet the four limbs of its shadow
Have no hatchet to pulverize the soul
Trust in thought, fictive tracing of an arc
Letting the homunculus arrive at a frightful abyss
Disproportionate height immobilizes a crippled organ
Trust in free will…far off in limitless time
Unknown matters will cause a betrayal
There is no one- and- only, just "3" carved on a huge rock
Trust in being blown along…in the arcane migration
Of 4D asterisms, it is only a matter of many or few
The dark universe is a storehouse of inscribed laws
Believe in metaphysical verticality…the iron in whiteness
But who can prove it? Or that over mankind's head

没有另一只手,双重看不见的存在
穿过金属的磁性,沿着肋骨的图案
在把棋子朝着更黑的水里移动……

There is not another hand, a doubly invisible entity
Through magnetism of metal, along the diagram of ribs
Moving the chess piece into even blacker water…

而我——又怎能不回到这里!

谁能理解我?或者说:我们
那是因为精神的传统,早已经
断奏,脐带上滴下的血
渗入泥土,发出黑色的吼叫

我回去,并不是寻找自己
那条泥泞的路,并不是唯一
只有丰饶的天空——信守诺言
直到今天,还为我指引方向

在这里,或许在河流之上
或许在火焰之上,或许在意识之上
虽然这一切都被割裂在昨天
但不可遏止的伤痛,依然还活着

已经不可能,再骑着马
在母语的疆域,独自巡游
泪光中的黄昏,恍若隔世
如此遥远,若隐若现……

从陌生的地方返回,我无意证明
我们死后,会有三个灵魂遗世

How Could I Not Want to Return Here!

Who can understand me or say why
This howl of blackness issues from us
For a spiritual tradition broken- off mid- note
For blood from a birth cord dripping into the dirt

I return, not to seek traces of my muddy road
There is more than that, because
Only the bounteous sky has stood by its promise
To give guidance, which I still may find

Above the rivers here, perhaps
Above flames, or even above consciousness
Although dismemberment happened yesterday
And the unstaunchable pain is still alive

No longer can I go off riding my own mount
To survey the rangeland of the mother tongue
A glance at twilight seems from another life
So far from me, at the edge of being visible

Returning from strange places, my intent is not to prove
That after death we leave three souls in this world

而我只是想,哪怕短暂地遗忘
那异化的身份,非人的声音。

选择祖先的方式,让游子回家
在这个金钱和物质的世纪
又有谁更在乎,心灵的感受
而作为一个人,我没有更高的祈求

我的灵魂,曾到过无数的地方
我看见他们,已经把这个地球——
糟蹋得失去了模样,而人类的非理性
迷途难返,现在还处于疯狂!

原谅我!已经无法再负重,因为
我的行囊里,没有别的任何东西。
因为我只想——也只有这样一个愿望:
用鼻子闻一闻,山坡上松针的清香……

在许多时候,骨骼的影子
把土墙上的痕迹抹去
金黄的口弦,不再诱惑我
另一个自我,已经客死在他乡!

但我还是要回去,这一决定——
不可更改,尽管我的历史和故乡的家园
已经伤痕累累,满目疮痍……
而我——又怎能不回到这里!

I wish to forget, if only for a short time
Alienation in my heart, inhuman sounds in my ears

If we prodigals choose the old ones' welcoming ways
Who in this world of money and stuff
Will give a fig for what draws our spirits on?
Yet as a person I have no higher wish

My soul has passed through many places
I have seen how people trample our earth
Almost beyond recognition, and human reason
Having strayed too far, gets caught up in mania!

Forgive me! I can no longer bear great burdens
Now all my personal luggage is gone
And I only keep a single wish in mind
To sniff the pure scent of pine needles on a slope...

Many are the times when images of skeletons
Rub away all traces of an earthen wall
A golden mouth harp can no longer lure me
My sojourning self has died away from home!

Still I want to return, and this decision
Cannot change, despite my history full of scars
And these eye- affronting sores all over my homeland
How could I not want to return here?

耶路撒冷的鸽子

在黎明的时候,我听见
在耶路撒冷我居住的旅馆的窗户外
一只鸽子在咕咕地轻哼……

我听着这只鸽子的叫声
如同是另一种陌生的语言
然而它的声音,却显得忽近忽远
我甚至无法判断它的距离
那声音仿佛来自地底的深处
又好像是从高空的云端传来

这鸽子的叫声,苍凉而古老
或许它同死亡的时间一样久远
就在离它不远的地方,在通往
哭墙和阿克萨清真寺的石板上
不同信徒的血迹,从未被擦拭干净
如果这仅仅是为了信仰,我怀疑
上帝和真主是否真的爱过我们

我听着这只鸽子咕咕的叫声
一声比一声更高,哭吧!开始哭!
原谅我,人类!此刻我只有长久的沉默……

A Dove of Jerusalem

At the hour of dawn, outside the window
Of the hotel where I stayed in Jerusalem
I heard a dove cooing ceaselessly

I was listening to this dove's call
Like one among several strange tongues
Yet the sound seemed now close by, now far
Its distance was hard for me to judge
As if it came from deep underground
Or reached my ears from cloudy heights

That dove's call was bleak and ageless
Perhaps equal in duration to death
In a place not far from it, on flagstones
That lead to Wailing Wall and Aqsa Mosque
Blood from different faiths has yet to be wiped clean
If merely for the sake of faith, then I wonder
Whether God and Allah have ever really loved us

I listen to the dove's coos reach a higher pitch
So wail then, let it break out wailing
Forgive me, fellow human beings, now I can only keep silent…

寻找费德里科·加西亚·洛尔加

我寻找你——
费德里科·加西亚·洛尔加
在格拉纳达的天空下
你的影子弥漫在所有的空气中
我穿行在你曾经漫步过的街道
你的名字没有回声
只有瓜达基维河①那轻柔的幻影
在橙子和橄榄林的头顶飘去
在格拉纳达,我虔诚地拜访过
你居住过的每一处房舍
从你睡过的婴儿时的摇篮
(虽然它已经停止了歌吟和晃动)
到你写作令人心碎的谣曲的书桌
费德里科·加西亚·洛尔加——
我寻找你,并不仅仅是为了寻找
因为你的生命和巨大的死亡
让风旗旋转的安达卢西亚
直到今天它的吉他琴还在鸣咽
因为你的灵魂和优雅的风度
以及喜悦底下看不见的悲哀
早已给这片绿色的土地盖上了银光
费德里科·加西亚·洛尔加——

In Search of Fredrico García Lorca

I go seeking you—
Frederico García Lorca
Beneath Granada's open skies
Your shadow pervades each draft of air
I pass along the avenues where you strolled
Your name brings no echo
Only watery gleams from Guadalquivir River[①]
Waver in the tops of orange and olive trees
In Granada, I devotedly pay visits
To every house you resided in
From the cradle you slept in as a baby
(Though its songs and rocking have stopped)
To the desk where you wrote heartrending ballads
Frederico García Lorca—
I go seeking you, not just to seek the Andalusia
Where flags were set tossing and twirling
By your life and gigantic death
And guitars go on weeping today
But because your soul and graceful manner
And the unseen sadness beneath your joy
Have covered this green land in silvery light
Frederico García Lorca—

一位真正的诗歌的通灵者,他不是
因为想成为诗人才来到这个世界上
而是因为通过语言和声音的通灵
他才成为一个真正的诗歌的酋长
费德里科·加西亚·洛尔加——
纵然你对语言以及文字的敏感
有着光一般的抽象和直觉
但你从来不是为了雕饰词语
而将神授的语言杀死的匠人
你的诗是天空的嘴唇
是泉水的渴望,是暝色的颅骨
是鸟语编的星星,是幽暗的思维
是蜥蜴的麦穗,是田园的杯子
是月桂的铃铛,是月亮的弱音器
是凄厉的晕光,是雪地上的磷火
是刺进利剑的心,是骷髅的睡眠
是舌尖的苦胆,是垂死的手鼓
是燃烧的喉咙,是被切开的血管
是死亡的前方,是红色的悲风
是固执的血,是死亡的技能
费德里科·加西亚·洛尔加——
只有真正到了你的安达卢西亚,我们
才会知道,你的诗为什么
具有鲜血的滋味和金属的性质!

①瓜达基维河,是一条流经诗人洛尔加故乡格拉纳达的河流。

A true clairvoyant of poetry, not just for the sake

Of becoming a poet did he come into this world

Yet only through mediumship of language and sound

Could he become a true chieftain of poetry

Frederico García Lorca—

Although your keen feeling for written words gave you

A light- like ability to extract the forms of things

With your God- given words you would never be

An artisan who drowned them in ornate displays

Your poems are lips of the open sky,

They are eagerness of springwater, cranium of dusk

They are stars in braided birdsong, thoughts in seclusion

They are wheat- ears known to crickets, pastoral cup

They are tiny bells of laurel, damper of moonlight

They are a chilly aureole, foxfire on snowy ground

Heart that stabs the sharp sword, sleep of a skeleton

Gall on the tongue- tip, tambourine at death's door

They are a throat on fire, a vein cut open

The front of death, the sad wind of redness

They are stubborn blood, skillfulness at dying

Frederico García Lorca—

At last we really made it to Andalusia

Only now do we know why your poetry holds

The taste of living blood, the gumption of metal!

①*The Guadalquivir River is the longest river in Lorca's home region of Andalusia.*

致尤若夫·阿蒂拉

你是不是还睡在
静静的马洛什河①的旁边？
或许你就如同
你曾描述过的那样——
只是一个疲乏的人，躺在
柔软的小草上睡觉。唉！
一个从不说谎，只讲真话的人
谁又能给你的心灵以慰藉呢？
因为饥饿，哪怕就是
神圣的泥土已经把你埋葬
但为了一片温暖的面包
你的影子仍然会在蒿尔托巴吉②
寻找一片要收割的成熟的庄稼
这时候，我们读你的诗
光明的词语会撞击我们的心
我们会这样想，怀着十分的好奇
你为什么能把人类的饥饿写到极致？
你的饥饿，不是你干瘪的胃吞噬的饥饿
不是那只饿得咯咯叫着的母鸡
你的饥饿，不是一个人的饥饿
不是反射性的饥饿，是没有记忆的饥饿
你的饥饿，是分成两半的饥饿

For Attila József

Are you still sleeping
By the quiet side of the Maros[1]?
Perhaps like someone you described
You may be just a worn- out man
Lying asleep on soft grass. Ah!
You who never told lies, spoke only truth
Who among us could console your spirit?
Owing to hunger, the soil has buried you
However sacred it may be
Yet for the warm gift of a loaf of bread
Your shadow may still be on Hortobagy Plain[2]
Seeking a crop that is now ripe for harvest
At such a time, as we read your poems
Words of light may strike our hearts
We may be curious to know how your pen
Could go right to the gist of human hunger?
Your hunger is not the hunger that gnaws
At your shrunken gut, not a clucking hungry hen
Your hunger is not the hunger of one person
Does not start chain reactions, or hold onto memories
Your hunger is hunger that splits into two halves
It is hunger of the victor and hunger of the conquered
It is the hunger of past, present and future
Your hunger is the hunger of a different kind of being

是胜利者的饥饿，也是被征服者的饥饿
是过去、现在和将来的饥饿
你的饥饿，是另一种生命的饥饿
没有饥饿能去证明，饥饿存在的本身
你的饥饿，是全世界的饥饿
它不分种族，超越了所有的国界
你的饥饿，是饿死了的饥饿
是发疯的铁勺的饥饿，是被饥饿折磨的饥饿
因为你的存在，那磨快的镰刀
以及农民家里灶炉中熊熊燃烧的柴火
开始在沉睡者的梦里闪闪发光
原野上的小麦，掀起一层层波浪
在那隐秘的匈牙利的黑土上面
你自由的诗句，正发出叮当的响声……

尤若夫·阿蒂拉——
我们念你的诗歌，热爱你
那是因为，从一开始直到死亡来临
你都站在不幸的人们一边！

①马洛什河，匈牙利南部的一条河流。
②蒿尔托巴吉，匈牙利大平原东北部的一片草原。

No hunger can prove the existence of hunger in itself

Your hunger is the hunger of this entire world

It is not divided by race, it is beyond national boundaries

Your hunger is the hunger of death by starvation

Hunger of a crazed iron ladle, hunger tortured by hunger

Because you existed, that sharpened sickle

And blazing wood in a farmer's kitchen stove

Sent their rays into a heavy sleeper's dream

Waves stirred through wheat on the plain

And over Hungary's hidden black soil

Your poetic lines of freedom rang forth…

Attila József—

Reading your poems, we love you warmly

Knowing you stood by the unfortunate ones

From the beginning until death's approaching

①*The Maros is a river in southern Hungary.*

②*The Hortobagy is a grassland located in the northwest area of Hungary's Great Plan.*

重新诞生的莱茵河

——致摄影家安德烈斯·古斯基[①]

让我们在这个地球上的某一处
或许就在任何一个地方

让我们像你一样
做一次力所能及的人为的创造

你镜头里的莱茵河
灰色是如此的遥远
看不见鸽子,天空没有飞的欲望
只有地平线,把缄默的心
镶入一只杯子

在镜头里,钢筋水泥的建筑
绽放着崭新的死亡
静止的阴影,再不会有鸟群
在这时空的咽喉中翻飞

你没有坐在河的岸边独自饮泣
你开始制着自己的作品
并果断地做出了如下的选择:

The Rhine River Reborn

—To the photographer Andreas Gursky[①]

Let us, at one spot on this globe
Any place at all would do

Let us bring about as you did
A man- made creation, as strength permits

In the Rhine River, seen through a lens
The grayness appears so remote
Doves are not seen, the sky has no urge to fly
Only the horizon, with hard- bitten heart
Embeds silence into a cup

Through the lens, structures of reinforced concrete
Put forth brand- new blossoms of death
Under still gloom, no flock will ever wheel and turn
In the throat of this particular locale

You did not sit on the bank and swallow tears
You went to work crafting your pieces
Resolutely choosing to do as follows:

把黑色的烟囱,从这里移走
并让钢筋水泥的隔膜,消失
在梦和现实的边界
你让两岸的大地和绿草生机勃勃
在天地之外也能听见鸟儿的鸣叫
是你与制造垃圾的人殊死搏斗
最终是用想象的利刃杀死了对方
你把莱茵河还给了自然……

①安德烈斯·古斯基(1955—),德国当代著名极简主义摄影家,环保主义者。

Move black smokestacks away from this place
Let the partitions of ribbed concrete disappear
At the boundary of dream and reality, along both banks
You let the land and its green grass spring to life
From another realm one's ears can catch birdsong
That is you in mortal struggle with makers of garbage
With imagination's blade slaying your adversary
Ultimately you give the Rhine back to nature...

①*Anreas Gursky (1955-) is an eminent German minimalist photographer and environmentalist.*

如果我死了……

如果我死了
把我送回有着群山的故土
再把我交给火焰
就像我的祖先一样
在火焰之上：
天空不是虚无的存在
那里有勇士的铠甲，透明的宝剑
鸟儿的马鞍，母语的盐
重返大地的种子，比豹更多的天石
还能听见，风吹动
荞麦发出的簌簌的声音
振翅的太阳，穿过时间的阶梯
悬崖上的蜂巢，涌出神的甜蜜
谷粒的河流，星辰隐没于微小的核心
在火焰之上：
我的灵魂，将开始远行
对于我，只有在那里——
死亡才是崭新的开始，灰烬还会燃烧
在那永恒的黄昏弥漫的路上
我的影子，一刻也不会停留
正朝着先辈们走过的路
继续往前走，那条路是白色的
而我的名字，还没有等到光明全部涌入
就已经披上了黄金的颜色：闪着光！

If I Should Die…

If I should die, send me back
To home ground, amid grouped mountains
Let me be given over to flames
Just as my ancestors were
Above flames, the open sky
Was never a realm of nothingness
Armor is there for the brave one, a precious see-through sword
Bird-traced saddle, salt of mother tongue, seed gone back to soil
Panthers and—more than that—celestial stones
There are susurrations to be heard
Made by wind blowing through buckwheat
The sun has taken wing, passing on time's staircase
Cliffside beehives ooze divine sweetness
A river of grain, star clusters hidden in tiny kernels
Above those flames
My soul will commence its journey
As for me, only in that place
Can death be a new start…embers burn again
On the road where eternal twilight gathers
My shadow will not pause even for an instant
Heading on the way my elders have walked
Continuing along that road of whiteness
And my name, before radiance comes to suffuse me
Being clothed in golden color, will give off rays!

巨石上的痕迹

——致 W. J. H. 铜像

原谅我,此次
不能来拜望另一个你
你早已穿过了——
那个属于死亡的地域
并不是在今天,你才又
在火焰的门槛前复活
其实你的名字,连同
那曾经发生的一切
无论是赞美,还是哑然
你的智慧,以及高大的身躯
都会被诺苏的子孙们记忆
是一个血与火的时代,选择了你
而作为一个彝人,你也竭尽了全力
在那块巨石上留下了痕迹
如同称职的工匠,你的铁锤
发出了叮当的声音,在那
黑暗与光明泥泞的路上
虽不是圣徒,却遮护着良心
你曾看见过垂直的天空上
阿什拉则①金黄的铜铃
那自然的法则,灼烫的词根

Marks on a Megalith
—for a bronze sculpture of W. J. H.

Forgive me, this is not the time

I cannot pay a visit to your other self

Who ventured forth some time ago

Into the realm where death claims all

Long before now you found resurrection

Through a flame- ringed threshold

In truth your name, with all it entails

Your doings praiseworthy or baffling

Your wisdom and your strapping physique

Will stay in the memories of Nuosu progeny

That era of fire and blood chose you

And as a Nuosu you did your utmost

To carve your mark upon a megalith

Like a handy craftsman, your hammer rang

Beside the road where people slogged

Through a quagmire of darkness and light

Though a layman, you gave sanctuary to conscience

Saw bronze bells from on high, wielded at prayer

By the sage Byashylaze[①], and you learned the word roots

Into which he had seared the laws of nature

只有群山才是永久的灵床
我知道,你从未领取过前往
——长眠之地的通行证
因为还在你健在的时候
我俩就曾经这样谈起——
我们活着已经不是为了自己
而死亡对于我们而言
仅仅是改变了方向的时间!

①阿什拉则,彝族古代著名的祭师、天象师、文字传承者。

We view yonder mountains as an ark to bear our souls

Yet I know you never pled for writ of passage

To be escorted there to take your eternal rest

Because you told me while still alive

We two are no longer living for ourselves

For us, death is only a change in direction

①*Biashylazzi was a ritualist and culture-bearer famous in the history of the Yi people.*

拉姆措湖①的反光

站在更高的地方,或许
这就是水的石板在反光
白天已经遁逝,天上的星群
涌入光明的牛奶
听不见神的脚步,在更高处
它们在冷冷地窥视大地
你说水的深度,在这里
还有什么更深的意义?
目光所及之处,可看见
碎银的穹顶,拉姆措
在瞬息间成了另一个
无法预测的未知的宇宙
浮现出了花豹的斑纹
也许在神秘的殿堂,祭祀
插出的金枝,那是银河
永恒不可颠覆的图像
我不是巫师,不能算出
词语的肋骨还能存活多久
但在这里,风吹透时间
没有了生和死的界线。肯定没有!
但那扇大门,看见了吧
却始终开着……

①拉姆措湖,青藏高原著名的神湖。

The Shimmers of Lamutso Lake[1]

Seen from a higher place, perhaps
The water's gleam may be a kind of paving stone
Day has withdrawn, and light of clustered stars
Trickles like milk through the sky
With unheard footsteps, in a higher place
The aloof gods peer down on the land
What a deeper meaning, pray tell
Might the depth of water hold there?
Wherever one's gaze wanders, a vault
Of pebbly silver meets the eye
Lamutso in a trice becomes
Another cosmos waiting to be fathomed
Where leopard- coat patterns are taking form
Perhaps seen within a sanctum, an offering place
Which proffers this golden bough, this chart showing
The unshakeable course of our Milky Way
I am not a shaman; it is not for me to divine
How long the ribs of language can enclose life
The wind here blows clean through time
The boundary of life and death has been effaced!
Yet a great door—don't you see it? —
Is standing forever open...

[1] *Lamutso Lake is a famous holy lake on the Qinghai-Tibet Plateau.*

致 酒

从不因悲愁而饮酒
那样的酒——
会让火焰与伤口
爬上死亡的楼梯
用酒来为心灵解忧
无色的桌布上
只会有更多的泪痕
我从来就只为欢聚
或许,还有倾诉
才去把杯盏握住
我从不一个人的时候
去品尝醉人的香醇
独有那真正的饮者
能理解什么是分享
我曾看见过牛皮的碗
旋转过众人的双手
既为活人也为死者
没有酒,这个世界
就不会有诗歌和箴言
黑暗与光明将更远
我相信,酒的能力
可消弭时间的距离

To Wine

In a gloomy mood I would never drink wine
Such wine would cause the wounded flames of a heart
To climb even higher onto death's ladder
Just try easing your blue mood with wine
You'll find that even more tears spatter
Upon the dull prospect of your tablecloth
As for me, I only take cup in hand
So I can be convivial, or perhaps
In a mood to exchange confidence
Never when alone do I sample
That intoxicating, mellow taste
Only a true drinker knows
The sharing of a bottle
I have seen leather bowls full of liquor
Making the rounds from hand to hand
They drank to the dead and to the living
If not for wine, in this world
There would be no poetry, no proverbs
Darkness and light would be further apart
It is my belief—the potency of wine
Can erase the distance of time

能忘掉反面的影子
但也唯有它,我们
最终才能沉落于无限
在浩瀚的天宇里
如同一粒失重的巨石
在把倒立的铁敲响……

It helps you forget the pull of the dark side
Yet it alone immerses you to infinite depth
In the sky's vast reaches
Like a boulder in free fall, resoundingly
You smite the inverted reflection of iron…

我接受这样的指令

我接受这样的指令：
不是拒绝冰
也不是排斥火焰
而是把冰点燃
让火焰成为冰……

A Command Accepted

I accept such a command
Neither to refuse ice
Nor to reject flames
But rather to set ice afire
To freeze flame within ice

契 约

每天早晨的醒来

都是被那个声音唤醒

除了我,还有所有的生命

如果有谁被遗忘

再听不见那个声音

并不是出了差错

那是永恒的长眠

偶然——找到了他!

Contract

Upon waking each morning
We are roused by a certain sound
Not just us, but all living things
If anyone is passed over
Without a chance to hear that sound
This is no mistake, the time has come
For eternal slumber
To catch up to that creature

鹰的葬礼

谁见过鹰的葬礼

在那绝壁上,或是

万丈瀑布的高空

宿命的铁锤

唯一的仪式

把钉子送上了穹顶

鹰的死亡,是粉碎的灿烂

是虚无给天空的

最沉重的一击!没有

送行者,只有太阳的

使臣,打开了所有的窗户……

The Eagle's Funeral

Who has seen the eagle's funeral
On a cliff or over a dizzying waterfall?
As it is nailed by fate's iron hammer
According to its one and only ritual
To the vault of heaven
The eagle's death is splendor in dispersal
Weightiest blow dealt by nothingness
Unto the sky, for which there are no
Senders- off; only emissaries
Of the sun, opening every window…

盲 人

暮年的博尔赫斯,在白昼
也生活在黑暗的世界,或许
他的耳朵,能延长光的手指
让最黑的部分也溢出亮度
当他独自仰着头的时候
脸上的微笑更是意味深长
不是词在构筑第四个空间
仍然是想象,在他干枯的眼底
浮现出一片黄金般的沙漠
他不是靠回忆,对比会杀死它们
那些透明的石头,没有重量的宫殿
并不完整的城堡,已经弯曲的钥匙
空悬在楼梯之上的图书和穹顶
没有边界的星空,倒置了的长椅
以及通向时间花园之外的小径
而这一切,都是被一个盲者创造
这是他用另一种语言打开的书籍
不为别人,这一次只为自己!

The Blind Man

Borges in his waning years, in the daylight
Living in a dark world, perhaps his ears can extend
Fingers of light, making the blackest places
Brim over with luminosity
Sitting alone with head thrown back
His face smiles over something deep in darkness
Words are not what built that fourth space
Always imagination; at the bottom of withered eyes
Where a golden stretch of sand comes in view
He does not depend on memory, for contrast is fatal
To those transparent stones, weightless palaces
That unfinished fortress, key already drooping
Bookshelves and vaulted ceilings hang in air
Starry sky with no boundaries, upended settee
And a path leading beyond time's garden
All of this, the creation of a blind man
A set of books opened by an alternate language
Not for others, but this time for himself

铜　像

半夜醒来，那时候
博尔赫斯已经习惯
要在黑暗中前行，独自
穿过客厅，一双手
摸索，凡是触摸到的
每一样东西，他都
十分熟悉，因为已经
没有更诱人的话题
能留住白天的思绪
独有死亡，一直追随
人到了这样的年龄
似乎没什么再可惧怕
只是每一次，当他
无意中摸到自己的头像
五根手指在更深的地方
便能感受到虚无的气息
那金属的冰凉，会让他
着实吓一跳，他不相信
那个铜像与自己有关
但他却知道，逝去的生命
已经在轮回的路上再不回头……

Bronze Bust

Waking late at night, Borges had gotten the habit
Of walking alone in the dark, passing through
His living room, groping his way forward
All objects in the house
Were familiar to his touch
For daylight topics held no allure
Nothing to occupy his thoughts at this hour
Death alone was his constant pursuer
When a man reaches such an age
It seems there is nothing more to fear
Yet every time he happened to touch
That bronze bust of his own head
His fingers could sense, somewhere deeper
A draft of emptiness, and he would take fright
At the metal's coldness, not believing
That bronze head had something to do with him
He knew this fleeting life had already set forth
Toward new lifetimes, and would never look back

流亡者

——写给诗人阿多尼斯和他流离失所的人民

那是一间老屋,与别人无关
只要流亡者活着——
它就活着,如果流亡者有一天
死了,它也许才会在亡者的记忆中被埋葬
假如亡灵永存,还会归来
它会迎接他,用谁也看不见的方式
虽然屋顶的一半,已经被炮弹损毁
墙壁上布满了无声的弹孔
流亡者的照片,还挂在墙上
一双双宁静的眼睛,沉浸在幽暗的
光线里,经过硝烟发酵的空气
仍然有烤羊肉和腌橄榄的味道
流亡者的记忆,会长时间停留在院落
那水池里的水曾被妈妈用作浇灌花草
娇艳硕大的玫瑰,令每一位
来访者动容,从茶壶中倒出的阿拉伯咖啡
和浓香的红茶,不知让多少异乡人体会过
款待他人的美德,虽然已经不能完全记住
是重逢还是告别?但那亲密的拥抱
以及嘴里发出的咂咂声响
却在回忆和泪眼里闪动着隐秘的事物
流亡者,并不是一个今天才有的称谓

THE EXILE

—For the poet Adonis and his uprooted countrymen

It is an old house and has nothing to do with others

Yet as long as the exile lives, it lives

Held in his memory, right up to

His dying day, perhaps to be buried with him,

Yet if departed souls endure, it will reappear

To greet him in a fashion no one sees

Though its roof be blown to pieces by shellfire

Its walls riddled with voiceless bullet holes,

Photos of loved ones still hang on its walls

Their eyes quiet in deepening twilight

Through reek of cordite, still wafting in the air,

Are smells of roast lamb and preserved olives,

The exile's memory hovers over that courtyard

Where flowers were watered from a pool by his mother

Raising gorgeous roses for guests to exclaim over,

And from that spout which poured Arabian coffee

And strong black tea, countless wayfarers were warmed

By hospitality, although memory no longer distinguishes

Reunions from partings. Now moist- eyed recollections

你们的祖先目睹过两河流域落日的金黄
无数的征服者都觊觎你麦香的乳房
当饥饿干渴的老人，在灼热的沙漠深处迷失
儿童和妇女在大海上，就只能选择
比生更容易的死的结局和未知
今天的流亡——并不是一次合谋的暴力
而是不同利益集团加害给无辜者的器皿
杯中盛满的只有绝望、痛哭、眼泪和鲜血
有公开的杀人狂，当然也有隐形的赌徒
被牺牲者——不是别人！
在叙利亚，指的就是没有被抽象过的
——活生生的千百万普通的人民
你看他们的眼神，那是怎样的一种眼神！
毫无疑问，它们是对这个世纪人类的控诉
被道义和良心指控的，当然不是三分之一
它包括指手画脚的极少数，沉默无语的大多数
就是那些无关痛痒的旁观者
我告诉你们，只要我们与受害者
生活在同一个时空——作为人！
我们就必须承担这份罪孽的某一个部分
那是一间老屋，与别人无关
然而，是的，的确，它的全身都布满了弹孔
就如同夜幕上死寂的星星……

2016. 7. 3

Of sipping sounds and embraces…retrieve hidden glimmers.
Long before today the title of exile fell upon your forebears
Who watched a golden day wane in the region of two rivers.
Countless conquerors lusted after its wheat- scented breasts,
Starving, thirsty elders went missing in scorching sands
While women and children, being taken over waves
Chose known death over an even- harsher life to come.
Today's exile is not the fruit of conspiracies to wreak violence
It is a vessel used by interest groups to harm innocent lives,
A cup filled with nothing but despair and blood and pain.
Bloodlust is public, yet those who wager in blood stay hidden,
So the ones who are sacrificed—in Syria
Can only be tens of thousands of ordinary citizens
Whose lives cannot be reduced to abstractions.
What is that look in their eyes? Just look and you will see
That is the accusatory gaze of 21st century humanity,
That indictment of conscience is not pointed at some small portion
It is directed at zealots, but also at the silent majority,
At the uninvolved ones who think they are only onlookers.
I can tell you: as long as we live in a common space
With those victims—as human beings
We must do our part in setting those wrongs right.
That is an old house, having nothing to do with others,
Yes indeed, its frame is riddled with bullet holes
Like deathly stars in the night firmament.

July 3, 2016

黑　色
——写给马列维奇①和我们自己

影子在更暗处，在潜意识的生铁里
它天空穹顶的幕布被道具遮蔽
唯一的出口，被形式吹灭的绝对
一粒宇宙的纤维，隐没在针孔的巨石
没有前行，更不会后退，无法预言风的方向
时间坠入无穷，只有一道消遁的零的空门
不朝向生，不朝向死，只朝向未知的等边
没有眼睛的面具，睡眠的灵床，看不见的梯子
被织入送魂的归途，至上的原始，肃穆高贵的维度
找不到开始，也没有结束，比永恒更悠久
光制造的重量，虚无深不可测，只抵达谜语的核心！

2016.7.5

①卡西米尔·塞·马列维奇（1878—1935），俄罗斯前卫艺术最重要的倡导者，20世纪具有世界影响的美术大师，其代表作《黑色正方形》已成为一种象征和标志。

Blackness

—For Malevich[1] and for ourselves

Shadow cast in dark places, in cast iron of the subconscious,
Curtain of that firmament unremarked behind stage props,
One and only exit, The Absolute extinguished by form,
Making neither advance nor retreat, not predictive of wind direction
Where time drops into infinity, just a receding empty gate of zero,
Not towards life or death, only towards the even-sided unknown,
Mask without eyes, bier of sleep, unseen ladder
Homeward path woven by chanted wake, arch-primordium, dimension of gravitas,
No beginning to be found, no conclusion, more enduring than forever
Weight fashioned by light, nothingness unfathomed, arriving at an enigma's heart!

June 5, 2016

①*Kazimir Malevich (1878—1935) was a key advocate of avant-garde art and a master artist of the 20th century. His representative work "Black Square" has become a touchstone and icon of modern art.*

金骏马

在草原的深处
它的呼吸如初
紫色的雾渐渐褪色
身体的曲线
融入无边的黑暗
反光的瞳仁摇曳
那是幽微的存在
没有星辰的翅膀
此时,停止了——
飞的欲望,四蹄脱落
避开引力的负担
重新返回了摇篮
无法擦去痕迹
皮毛被晶液浸透
那是天空和宇宙——
不可被分割的部分
唯有一声响鼻传来
超然于外,燧石的语言
不会被遗忘的记忆
脊骨的弧线弯曲
等待成为闪电的一刻
只有当黎明的曙光
再次来临的时候

Golden Steed

Deep in the grassland
It draws breath as at the origin.
Violet mists gradually fade
And contours of its body
Melt into boundless darkness.
Wavering reflections from pupils
Are signs of its tenebrous presence.
Constellations no longer serve for wings,
At this moment the urge to fly
Comes to a stop—its hooves are shed.
It gives the slip to gravity's burden
Returns again to its cradle.
Its hair bears traces not to be effaced
Suffused with crystalline substance
Which is its inalienable share
Of the sky and the cosmos.
Its long neigh floats on still air
Sublimely outside, language of flint,
Memory that won't be forgotten,
Curve of the backbone flexing
Ready for the moment of lightning.
Only when pale light of dawn
Makes its advent once again

它的踢踏声,才会
敲响这大地的鼓面
那幻象的影子,黄金一般
在地平线上忽隐忽现……

          2016. 7. 5

Will the tattoo of those hoofbeats

Sound on the drumhead of this land.

That half- real shape, a golden streak

Appears and disappears on the horizon.

                                                                 June 5, 2016

刺穿的心脏

——写给吉茨安·尤斯金诺维奇·塔比泽[①]

你已经交出了被刺穿的心脏
没有给别人，而是你的格鲁吉亚
当我想象穆赫兰山[②]顶雪的反光
你的面庞就会在这大地上掠过

不知道你的尸骨埋在何处
那里的白天和黑夜是否都在守护
在你僵硬地倒毙在山冈之前
其实你的诗已经越过了死亡地带

对于你而言，我是一位不速之客
然而我等待你却已经很久很久
为了与你相遇，我不认为这是上苍的安排
更不会去相信，这是他人祈祷的结果

那是你的诗和黑暗中的眼泪
它们并没有死，那悲伤的力量
从另一个只有同病相怜者的通道
送到了我一直孤单无依的心灵

即使你已经离世很久，但你的诗
依然被复活的角笛再次吹响

Your Pierced Heart

—For Titsian Tabidze[1]

You have rendered up your pierced heart
Not to another soul, but to the land of Georgia.
While envisioning sunlight on Meskheti's[2] snowy peaks
I see shifting traces of your features on the land.

I know not where your remains are buried
Or if daylight and nighttime watch over you there,
Before you keeled over stiffly on a hilltop
Your poems had made it across the death zone.

For you, I may be an unexpected guest
But I have been waiting for someone like you,
To me this meeting was arranged by powers above
I will never attribute it to intercession by others.

It was through your poems…your tears in darkness
By no means dead, that your power to face sorrow
Was delivered to this heart with nobody to lean upon
By means of someone who could only commiserate.

Though you left this world years ago, your poetry
Still sounds the clarion call of resurrection.

相信我——我们是这个世界的同类
否则就不会在幽暗的深处把我惊醒

我们都是群山和传统的守卫者
为了你的穆哈姆巴吉③和我祖先的克哲④
勇敢的死亡以及活下去所要承受的痛苦
无非都是生活和命运对我们的奖赏……

2016.7.5

①吉茨安·尤斯金诺维奇·塔比泽（1895—1937），20世纪格鲁吉亚和苏联著名诗人，象征主义诗歌流派的领袖人物。1937年去世，是苏联大清洗牺牲者之一，死后平反恢复名誉。
②穆赫兰山，格鲁吉亚境内一座著名的山脉。
③穆哈姆巴吉，格鲁吉亚一种古老的诗歌形式。
④克哲，彝族一种古老的诗歌对唱形式。

Believe me—kindred soul of mine in this world
What else could rouse me amidst such darkness?

We both watch over mountain ranges and traditions
For the sake of yourmuhamubaji ③ and my flytings④
The pain we undergo to die bravely or to go on living
Is surely our reward, dealt out by fate and life!

July 5, 2016

① *Titsian Tabidze (1895—1937) was a famous 20th century poet of Georgia and the former Soviet Union. Having emerged as a leader of the Symbolist School, he was fell victim to the Great Purge of 1937. His good name was vindicated after his death.*

② *Meskheti is a range of mountains in Georgia.*

③ *Muhamubaji is a traditional form of folk poetry in Georgia.*

④ *Kneprep (rendered here by the Scottish word "flyting") is a duel of poetic, proverbial language between two speakers. Kneprep contests are held at weddings, clan gatherings and other celebratory occasions by the Yi people in Daliang Mountains.*

诗人的结局

我不知道,
是 1643 年的冬天,
还是 1810 年彝族过年的日子。

总之,实际上,
老人们都这样说。

在吉勒布特,
那是一场罕见的大雪,
整整下了一天一夜。
住在这里的一家人,
有十三个身强力壮的儿子,
他们骄傲的父母,
都用老虎和豹子,
来为他们的后代命名。

鹰的影子穿过了,
谚语谜一般的峡谷。

大雪还在下,
直到傍晚的时候,
妈妈在嘴里喃喃地
数着一个个归来的儿子。

The Outcome of a Poet

It could have been in the year 1643
Or perhaps in the year 1810
On New Year's Day by the Nuosu calendar.

It happened in traditional times,
All the old people speak of it.

There was a huge snowfall
Seldom seen in Jjile Bute
Snow fell all day and all night.
A family that lived there
Had thirteen sturdy sons.
Their parents gave each of them
A tiger- name or leopard- name,
To show pride in their progeny.

The eagle's shadow passed over
The ancient riddle of that deep gorge.

The snow kept falling
Until the hour of twilight
Their mother's murmuring voice
Counted off her returning sons:

"一个、两个、三个……"

她站在院落外,
看着自己的儿子们,
披着厚实的羊毛皮毡,
全身冒着热气。
透过晶莹的雪花,
她的眼睛闪动着光亮。

这一切都发生在这里。

一块破碎的锅庄石,
被坚硬的犁头惊醒,
时间已经是 2011 年春季,
他们用手指向那里:

"你的祖先就居住在此地!"

燃烧的牛皮在空中弯曲成文字。

一个词语的根。
一个谱系的火焰。
被捍卫的荣誉。
黑色的石骨。
从鹰爪未来的杯底,
传来群山向内的齐唱。
太阳的钟点,

"One…that's two…and that's three…"

She stood at the courtyard gate
Watching her sons file in
Emanating warm vapors
Wool capes on their shoulders
Flecked with crystalline flakes
Making their mother's eyes shine.

All of this happened in that place.

A broken hearthstone was dug up,
Roused by the hard tip of a plow,
That was in springtime of 2011,
People pointed to the place:

"Your ancestors lived right here."

Cowhide burning in midair bends into words

The root of a word- group,
The flame of a family tree,
Family honor defended,
Black osseous rocks.
From within an eagle talon cup, into this future
Comes the inward chant of ranged mountains,
Hour points of the sun

从未停止过旋转。

我回到了这里。
戏剧刚演到第三场。

因为父子连名的传统,
那结局我已知晓。
从此死亡对于我而言,
再不是一个最后的秘密。
这不是一场游戏,
作为主角,不要耻笑我,
我是另一个负重的虚无,
戏的第七场已经开始……

2016.7.7

Never halted their spinning course.

At the hour that I returned there
The drama was in its third act.

Due to tradition that links fathers' and sons' names
I know what the outcome will be.
The coming of death, as I see it
Is no longer the ultimate secret.
This is not a game, and as protagonist
I am not to be ridiculed, if you please.
I am a form of nothingness that bears burdens,
The seventh act of the drama has begun...

July 7, 2016

致叶夫图申科[①]

对于我们这样的诗人：
忠诚于自己的祖国，
也热爱各自的民族。
然而我们的爱，却从未
被锁在狭隘的铁笼，
这就如同空气和阳光，
在这个地球的任何一个地方，
都能感受到它的存在。
我们或许都有过这样的经历，
都曾为另一个国度发生的事情流泪，
就是他们的喜悦和悲伤，
虽然相隔遥远，也会直抵我们的心房，
尽管此前我们是如此的陌生。
如果说我们的诞生，是偶然加上的必然，
那我们的死亡，难道不就是必然减去的偶然吗？
朋友，对于此我们从未有过怀疑！

2016.7.7

[①] 叶·亚·叶夫图申科（1933— ），苏联俄罗斯诗人。他是苏联五十年代末、六十年代初"大声疾呼"派诗人的代表人物，也是二十世纪最具影响力的诗人之一。他的诗题材广泛，以政论性和抒情性著称，既写国内现实生活，也干预国际政治，以"大胆"触及"尖锐"的社会问题而闻名。

For Yevtushenko[1]

For poets like ourselves, though each
Be loyal to his own Motherland,
Devoted to his own nationality,
Love will never be a something
To be locked in a narrow cage,
For it is like air and sunlight,
From any spot on this earth
You can feel its existence.
We have both experienced sudden tears
For what happened in another country;
Their griefs and joyful times, though distant
Often find their way into our hearts,
Though we thought them strangers.
If our births be necessity built upon randomness
Won't our deaths be randomness shorn of necessity?
My friend, we have never been in doubt of this!

July 7, 2016

①*Yevgeny Aleksandrovich Yevtushenko (born 1933) is a Soviet/Russian poet who was a representative figure of the Russian "New Wave" and a major world poet. His subjects ranged from personal lyricism to political issues, which he was able to view from an international perspective. He boldly involved himself in international political affairs and grappled with sensitive social matters.*

没有告诉我

比阿什拉则①,
没有告诉我,
在灵魂被送走的路上,
是否还有被款待的机会。
有人说无论结果怎样,
你都要带上自己的木勺。
我有两把木勺,
一把是最长的,还有一把是最短的,
但这样的聚会却经常是
不长不短的木勺,
才能让赴宴者舀到食物,
但是我没有,这是一个问题。

2016.7.8

①比阿什拉则,彝族历史上最著名的祭司和文字传承掌握者,以超度和送魂闻名。

Not Told

Biashylazzi did not tell me[1]
If more rich entertainments await me
Along the road for sending off souls.
Some people say that just in case
Each soul should bring his own spoon.
As for me, I have two wooden spoons,
One's handle is the longest, one the shortest,
But in such gatherings it often happens
A spoon neither long nor short is needed
To ladle morsels into a diner's mouth.
I must live with the fact—that spoon is not mine.

July 8, 2016

[1] *Biashylazzi was an ancient sage of the Nusou people to whom is attributed the invention of the Yi writing system.*

谁也不能高过你的头颅

——献给屈原[1]

诗人！光明的祭司，黑暗的对手
没有生，也没有死，只有太阳的
光束，在时间反面的背后
把你的额头，染成河流之上
沉默的金黄。你的车轮旋转
如岩石上的风暴，你孑然而立
望着星河深处虚无的岸边
谁也不能高过你的头颅
你饮木兰上的露水，不会饥饿
每一次自我的放逐，词语的
骨笛，都会被火焰吹响
谁也不能高过你的头颅
因为在群山的顶部，你的吟游
如同光明的馈赠，这个世界
不会再有别人——不会！
能像真正的纯粹的诗人一样
像一个勇士，独自佩戴着蕙草
去完成一个人与众神的合唱
谁也不能高过你的头颅
只有太阳神，那公正无私的双手
能为你戴上自由的——冠冕！
诗人！只有你的命令能抵达
并阻止死神的来临，那高脚杯

No One Can Overshadow Your Skull
—Dedicated to Qu Yuan[①]

Poet, priest of light and foe of darkness!
For you there is neither birth nor death, only rays
Of sunlight, from behind the far side of time
Casting the quiet gleam of a golden river
On your brow. Your chariot wheels spin
Like storm winds around a boulder; you loom
Eyes turned toward Star River's far bank of nothingness
None of us could overshadow your skull
You are fortified against hunger by magnolia dew
At each self-banishment, your flame leaps up
To aspirate anew the bone-flute of language
None of us could overshadow your skull
For your troubadourage on mountaintops
Has showered us with largess of radiance
Such as no other could confer, none ever
Could play such a true, pure poet's part
Like a lone warrior, decked with angelica sprigs
Off to sing in chorus with a whole pantheon
None of us could overshadow your skull
Only Helios with his just, impartial hands
Could place the crown of freedom on your head
Only your command reaches the Grim Reaper
And can forestall his coming, at the hour

盛满了菊花酿造的美酒
那是宴客的时辰,被唤醒的神灵
都会集合在你的身后,仰望
天河通向未知的渡口,你手中的
火把,再一次照亮了黑暗的穹顶
它的颜色超过了所有我们见过的白昼
只有你的云车不用铁的铠甲
和平养育的使者,人群中的另类
只有你能说出属于自己的语言
无论是在人的面前,还是在神的殿堂
你都紧握着真理和道德的权杖
谁也不能高过你的头颅
当你呼唤日月、星辰与河流
它们的应答之声,就会飘浮在
肃穆寂寥的天庭——并成为绝响!
我不知道,难道还有别的声音
能具有这般非凡的超自然的力量
说你没有生,也没有死
那是因为你永远行走在轮回的路上
就是你那所谓最后的消遁
也仅仅是一种被死亡命名的形式
诗人!如果有生的权利,当然
你也会有死的权利,但是——
唯有你,在死亡降临的瞬间
就已经用另一种方式完成了复活
由此,我们曾愚钝地寻找过你
其实你就是这片母语的土地
和神圣的天空,我们的每一次呼吸
都能感受到你的存在,你是
流动的空气,一只飞翔的鸟

For feting guests, when goblets are filled
With floral ambrosia, and awakened deities
Gather behind to gaze with you at the Sky River
Toward the ford of the unknown, with torch in hand
Illuminating the vault of darkness with colors
That surpass any daylight spectrum we know
Only your cloud- chariot needs no armor
Messenger reared in peace, exception from the crowd
Only you could speak in your own language
Both before human beings and in divine counsels
You firmly grip the scepter of truth and virtue
None of us could overshadow your skull
As you invoke rivers and luminaries of the sky
Their answering resonances soon hang in midair
Brought to culmination in heaven's solemn sanctum!
What other voice possesses such supernal force?
For you there is neither birth nor death, because
You eternally traverse the road of recurrence
And your so- called final disappearance
Was merely a form designated by death
Poet! Since you were entitled to be born
You are entitled to your death, and yet
By the time death descended upon you
Your rebirth had been realized in another guise
In truth you are the soil of this mother tongue
And its sacred sky, so we sense your existence
In every breath we draw. You are
In currents of air, in the flight of a bird

没有名字的一株幽兰，树叶上的昆虫
一块谁也无法撼动的巨石，或许
就是一粒沙漏中落下的宇宙
谁也不能高过你的头颅
在一个种族集体的记忆里
作为诗人，你是第一个，没有并列
用自己的名字，开启了一条诗歌的航道
你不会死去，因为你的不朽和牢不可破
诗歌纵然已经伤痕累累，但直到今天——
它也从未放弃过对生命的歌唱！

            2016年5月28日凌晨

①屈原（公元前340年—公元前278年），中国历史上第一位伟大的爱国诗人，中国浪漫主义文学的奠基人，被誉为"中华诗祖"。

A hidden unnamed orchid, insect on a leaf
A boulder that no one can dislodge, or even
The grain of a cosmos falling in an hourglass
None of us could overshadow your skull
In the collective memory of a race you were first
In your own name, without parallel
To initiate a flight path for future poetry
Because of your undying, unshakeable strength
Right up to today, despite being riddled with scars
Poetry has never stopped singing the song of life!

May 28, 2016

①*Qu Yan (340-278 B. C.) is known to history as a patriot and as the first poet who laid the foundation for romantic literature. He has been given the title "Progenitor of Chinese Poetry."*

我，雪豹……

——献给乔治·夏勒[①]

1

流星划过的时候
我的身体，在瞬间
被光明烛照，我的皮毛
燃烧如白雪的火焰
我的影子，闪动成光的箭矢
犹如一条银色的鱼
消失在黑暗的苍穹
我是雪山真正的儿子
守望孤独，穿越了所有的时空
潜伏在岩石坚硬的波浪之间
我守卫在这里——
在这个至高无上的疆域
毫无疑问，高贵的血统
已经被祖先的谱系证明
我的诞生——
是白雪千年孕育的奇迹
我的死亡——
是白雪轮回永恒的寂静
因为我的名字的含义：

I, Snow Leopard...

—Dedicated to George Schaller[1]

1

As a meteor parts the sky overhead

My body, in an instant

Is touched by radiance

Set alight in snow- white flames

And my shape is a lightning streak

Like a silvery fish receding

Against the dark vault of sky

I am the true son of snowy mountains

Watching over solitude, persisting

Through all temporal stages

Crouched among hardened waves of boulders

I stand guard here—

On this rangeland of supreme height

Surely my blood has been proven noble

By the line of descent from my forefathers

My birth was a miracle

Gestated for millennia in white snow

My death is cyclic transformation

Of silence in this snowy domain

Just as my name implies

我隐藏在雾和霭的最深处
我穿行于生命意识中的
另一个边缘
我的眼睛底部
绽放着呼吸的星光
我思想的珍珠
凝聚成黎明的水滴
我不是一段经文
刚开始的那个部分
我的声音是群山
战胜时间的沉默
我不属于语言在天空
悬垂着的文字
我仅仅是一道光
留下闪闪发亮的纹路
我忠诚诺言
不会被背叛的词语书写
我永远活在
虚无编织的界限之外
我不会选择离开
即便雪山已经死亡

2

我在山脊的剪影,黑色的
花朵,虚无与现实
在子夜的空气中沉落

自由地巡视,祖先的
领地,用一种方式

I hide in mist and windborne frost
I too walk in awareness of life
But skirting its other margin
Blooming from deep in my eyes
Is the starry glint of breath
The pearls of my thought
Coalesce into droplets of dawn
In a long chapter of scripture
I am not the opening lines
Ranged mountains defeat time by silence
Which is also my voice
I do not belong to those written words
Suspended by language from the sky
I am merely a beam of light
That leaves a radiant tracery
I faithfully vow
No traitorous words will ever inscribe me
I forever live beyond boundaries
That some would fashion without substance
I will never choose to leave here
Even when death claims these snowy peaks

2

On the cutout of a ridgeline, I stand as a flower
Of deeper black, as substance and nothingness
Fall away in the air of midnight

In freedom patrolling this territory
Of my forefathers, by a pattern passed down

那是骨血遗传的密码

在晨昏的时光,欲望
就会把我召唤
穿行在隐秘的沉默之中

只有在这样的时刻
我才会去,真正重温
那个失去的时代……

3

望着坠落的星星
身体漂浮在宇宙的海洋
幽蓝的目光,伴随着
失重的灵魂,正朝着
永无止境的方向上升
还没有开始——
闪电般地纵身一跃
充满强度的脚趾
已敲击着金属的空气
谁也看不见,这样一个过程
我的呼吸、回忆、秘密的气息
已经全部覆盖了这片荒野
但不要寻找我,面具早已消失……

4

此时,我就是这片雪域

In code of blood and bone

In glimmering pre- dawn hours
Heeding the call of appetite
I wend my silent, secret way

Only in such moments
Do I truly bring alive
An epoch that seemed to have passed…

3

Watching a falling star
This body drifts in a cosmic sea
Eye- glint of ghostly blue keeps company
With a weightless soul, as they ascend
Toward ever- higher levels
Before the body even starts
To clear the ground with lightning leap
Those legs filled with tensile strength
Strike up a beat on metallic air
In a series of movements no one sees
My breath and memories and secret scent
By now cover this wilderness, but do not seek me
Where all traces of masks are gone

4

Now, I myself am none other than this snowy realm

从吹过的风中,能聆听到
我骨骼发出的声响
一只鹰翻腾着,在与看不见的
对手搏击,那是我的影子
在光明和黑暗的
缓冲地带游离
没有鸟无声的降落
在那山谷和河流的交汇处
是我留下的暗示和符号
如果一只旱獭
拼命地奔跑,但身后
却看不见任何追击
那是我的意念
已让它感到了危险
你在这样的时刻
永远看不见我,在这个
充满着虚妄、伪善和杀戮的地球上
我从来不属于
任何别的地方!

5

我说不出所有
动物和植物的名字
但这是一个圆形的世界
我不知道关于生命的天平
应该是,更靠左边一点
还是更靠右边一点,我只是
一只雪豹,尤其无法回答

Move quietly and listen into the wind
You may hear the crack of my joints stretching
An eagle riding updrafts does combat
With an unseen rival—that is my shadow
Which ranges over the threshold zone
Between light and darkness
Where a valley meets with a river's course
No bird of prey makes its silent plunge
I have left this as a sign for you to read
If a marmot scrambles for cover
Even where no pursuer
Is seen running behind it
That is due to my intention
Which makes it sense the presence of danger
At such times you will not see me
On this globe rife with pretense and slaughter
You will never find me
In any domain but my own

5

I cannot tell you the name
Of this plant or that animal
Yet I am sure this is a circular world
I know not if the weight on life's scale
Should be nudged a bit to the right
Or nudged a bit to the left
I am just a snow leopard, unable to tell you
The relation of one living thing to another

这个生命与另一个生命的关系
但是我相信，宇宙的秩序
并非来自于偶然和混乱
我与生俱来——
就和岩羊、赤狐、旱獭
有着千丝万缕的依存
我们不是命运——
在拐弯处的某一个岔路
而更像一个捉摸不透的谜语
我们活在这里已经很长时间
谁也离不开彼此的存在
但是我们惊恐和惧怕
追逐和新生再没有什么区别……

6

我的足迹，留在
雪地上，或许它的形状
比一串盛开的
梅花还要美丽
或许它是虚无的延伸
因为它，并不指明
其中的奥妙
也不会预言——
未知的结束
其实生命的奇迹
已经表明，短暂的
存在和长久的死亡
并不能告诉我们

But I believe: The order of the cosmos

Does not come from random confusion

Innate with me from birth

Are a thousand threads of reliance

With antelope, red fox and marmot

We are not a bypath where fate turns a corner

We are more like a riddle beyond solving

We have lived here a long time already

Now none can do without the other's existence

Yet we must face startlement and fear

Between the hunt and a new life there is no longer a distinction…

6

My tracks left on snowy ground

Have shapes that to some

May have greater beauty

Than a string of plum blossoms

Or they may be extensions of nothingness

Because they point out nothing

About any inherent mystery

And cannot prophesy

A conclusion still unknown

In truth the miracle of life

Has made it clear: Between transitory life

And death that lasts forever

There is no way of telling

它们之间谁更为重要？
这样的足迹，不是
占卜者留下的，但它是
另一种语言，能发出
寂静的声音
唯有起风的时刻，或者
再来一场意想不到的大雪
那些依稀的足迹
才会被一扫而空……

7

当我出现的刹那
你会在死去的记忆中
也许还会在——
刚要苏醒的梦境里
真切而恍惚地看见我：
是太阳的反射，光芒的银币
是岩石上的几何，风中的植物
是一朵玫瑰流淌在空气中的颜色
是一千朵玫瑰最终宣泄成的瀑布
是静止的速度，黄金的弧形
是柔软的时间，碎片的力量
是过度的线条，黑色+白色的可能
是光铸造的酋长，穿越深渊的0
是宇宙失落的长矛，飞行中的箭
是被感觉和梦幻碰碎的
某一粒逃窜的晶体
水珠四溅，色彩斑斓

Which is more important
These traces left by paws
Are not marks of a diviner
Yet they are a language, able to pronounce
The voice of silence
Until a stiff wind bears down
Or a snowstorm steals up
Then this line of fading prints
Will be swept from existence...

7

At the instant I appear
I may recur, out of once- dead memory
Or in a dream vision newly wakened
You will glimpse me, genuine yet set apart
I am the sun's reflection, beam from silver coins
Geometry among boulders, planted in wind
The color of roses trickling through air
Cataract giving release to a thousand roses
Speed in stillness, golden arc
Strokable time, force from brokenness
Incremental contour, black + white made possible
Chieftain stamped in light, ' 0' that crosses the abyss
Dropped spear of the cosmos, arrow in flight
A fugitive crystal split away
From wishful dream visions
Flung water- beads, mottled coloring

是勇士佩带上一颗颗通灵的贝壳
是消失了的国王的头饰
在大地子宫里的又一次复活

8

二月是生命的季节
拒绝羞涩，是燃烧的雪
泛滥的开始
野性的风，吹动峡谷的号角
遗忘名字，在这里寻找并完成
另一个生命诞生的仪式
这是所有母性——
神秘的词语和诗篇
它只为生殖之神的
降临而吟诵……

追逐　离心力　失重　闪电　弧线
欲望的弓　切割的宝石　分裂的空气
重复的跳跃　气味的舌尖　接纳的坚硬
奔跑的目标　颌骨的坡度　不相等的飞行
迟缓的光速　分解的摇曳　缺席的负重
撕咬　撕咬　血管的磷　齿唇的馈赠
呼吸的波浪　急遽的升起　强烈如初
捶打的舞蹈　临界死亡的牵引　抽空　抽空
想象　地震的战栗　奉献　大地的凹陷
向外渗漏　分崩离析　喷泉　喷泉　喷泉
生命中坠落的倦意　边缘的颤抖　回忆

Telepathic cowries decking a warrior's sash
A king's headpiece gone missing
Again resurrected in the planet's womb

8

February is the season of life saying no to shyness
Commences the rampage of burning snow
A wanton wind, blowing its trumpet in a gorge
Forgetting names, here seeks and completes
The ceremony for another life to be born
The mysterious psalmody
Of all that is motherly
Coming forth and lifting her voice
Only for the god of fertility…

Hot pursuit…decentering force…free- fall…lightning flash…arcing
Desire's bow…well- split gem…unresisting air
Exact same leap…tongue tip of scent…hardness for the receptive
Sprint and goal…slope of jaw…unequalled flying
Lingering light- beam…tug of dissolution…burden of absence
Jaws clamping…worrying…phosphor of veins…toothsome gift
Waves of respiration…abrupt ascent…intensity like the start
Hammering dance…death's tug at the edge…emptying…emptying
Imaginings…earthquake tremors…offering made…concavity of earth
Percolating outward … collapse in pieces … fountain … fountain … fountain…
Fallen through to weariness in life … edge- walker's tremble … remembrance

雷鸣后的寂静　等待　群山的回声……

9

在峭壁上舞蹈
黑暗的底片
沉落在白昼的海洋
从上到下的逻辑
跳跃虚无与存在的山涧
自由的领地
在这里只有我们
能选择自己的方式
我的四肢攀爬
陡峭的神经
爪子踩着岩石的
琴键，轻如羽毛
我是山地的水手
充满着无名的渴望
在我出击的时候
风速没有我快
但我的铠甲在
空气中嘶嘶发响
我是自由落体的王子
雪山十二子的兄弟
九十度地往上冲刺
一百二十度地骤然下降
是我有着花斑的长尾
平衡了生与死的界限……

Stillness after lightning...waiting...echoes from mountains

9

Skipping along a cliff- edge
In the film- negative of darkness
Sinking from sight in daylight's sea
Top to bottom logic of descent
Leaps the ravine of existence and nothingness
Territory of freedom
Where we are the only ones
To choose our own way
My four limbs clamber
Up the nerve net of a precipice
Paws treading on piano keys
Of boulders, with feather- light moves
I am a sailor of high terrain
Filled with wishes you cannot name
At the moment I strike
The wind's speed cannot rival mine
Yet I have armor all around me
It is heard sighing as air currents blow in
I am the prince of free- falling objects
Brother among twelve tribes of snow country
Charging upward at 90 degrees
Or in rapid descent at 120 degrees
It is my long, spotted tail that balances me
Just short of death's edge...

10

昨晚梦见了妈妈
她还在那里等待,目光幽幽

我们注定是——
孤独的行者
两岁以后,就会离开保护
独自去证明
我也是一个将比我的父亲
更勇敢的武士
我会为捍卫我高贵血统
以及那世代相传的
永远不可被玷污的荣誉
而流尽最后一滴血

我们不会选择耻辱
就是在决斗的沙场
我也会在临死前
大声地告诉世人
——我是谁的儿子!
因为祖先的英名
如同白雪一样圣洁
从出生的那一天
我就明白——
我和我的兄弟们
是一座座雪山

10

Last night I dreamed of Mama
She is still waiting there, that uncanny look in her eyes

We are fated to be
Wayfarers in solitude
After two years it was time to venture forth
To prove in my own way
I could someday be a warrior
Fighting bigger battles than my father
In defense of my noble bloodline
And of honor that was kept unstained
Down through generations
Let my last drop of blood be shed

I will never choose a path of shame
At the fatal scene of all- out battle
Before I meet my death
I will loudly tell the world
Whose son I am!
And that my forefathers' heroic names
Have the holy purity of snow
From the day of my birth
I already understood
That my brothers and I
Would forever be guardian deities

永远的保护神

我们不会遗忘——
神圣的职责
我的梦境里时常浮现的
是一代代祖先的容貌
我的双唇上飘荡着的
是一个伟大家族的
黄金谱系!
我总是靠近死亡,但也凝视未来

11

有人说我护卫的神山
没有雪灾和瘟疫
当我独自站在山巅
在目光所及之地
白雪一片清澈
所有的生命都沐浴在纯净的
祥和的光里。远方的鹰
最初还能看见,在无际的边缘
只剩下一个小点,但是,还是同往常一样
在蓝色的深处,消失得无影无踪
在不远的地方,牧人的炊烟
袅袅轻升,几乎看不出这是一种现实
黑色的牦牛,散落在山凹的低洼中
在那里,会有一些紫色的雾霭,漂浮
在小河白色冰层的上面
在这样的时候,灵魂和肉体已经分离

Of each snow peak

I will never forget
This sacred calling
In dreams floating before me
A chain of faces stretches far back
And from between my lips
Reverberates the golden genealogy
Of a grand family line
I always verge upon death, yet keep eyes on the future

11

Some say the mountain god I serve
Inflicts no plagues or snow disasters
Standing by myself on a peak
Whichever way I turn
My eyes are met by pristine snow
All creatures are bathed in pure, benign light
And a distant eagle dwindles
A watcher whose eyes follow that dot
At some point loses track in blue depths
Not too far below, cooking smoke of herdsmen
Wafts upward, hardly suggesting the workaday world
Black yaks are peppered about in boggy hollows
Down there a bluish haze floats
Over rime- ice of a small river
At such times, spirit and flesh go their own ways

我的思绪，开始忘我地漂浮
此时，仿佛能听到来自天宇的声音
而我的舌尖上的词语，正用另一种方式
在这苍穹巨大的门前，开始
为这一片大地上的所有生灵祈福……

12

我活在典籍里，是岩石中的蛇
我的命是一百匹马的命，是一千头牛的命
也是一万个人的命。因为我，隐蔽在
佛经的某一页，谁杀死我，就是
杀死另一个看不见的，成千上万的我
我的血迹不会留在巨石上，因为它
没有颜色，但那样仍然是罪证
我销声匿迹，扯碎夜的帷幕
一双熄灭的眼，如同石头的内心一样隐秘
一个灵魂独处，或许能听见大地的心跳？
但我还是只喜欢望着天空的星星
忘记了有多长时间，直到它流出了眼泪

13

一颗子弹击中了
我的兄弟，那只名字叫白银的雪豹
射击者的手指，弯曲着
一阵沉闷的牛角的回声
已把死亡的讯息传遍了山谷
就是那颗子弹

I am absorbed in my unwinding thought-trains
Now sounds from the firmament seem audible
Here at this giant portal leading to the sky-vault
Words on my tongue tip, after their own fashion
Begin praying for all creatures on this land

12

I also live in classic texts, called 'snake among crags'
My life is worth a hundred horses, a thousand cows
Even ten thousand humans, for a verse
Hidden in a scripture says, whoever kills me
Kills an unseen me that takes a thousand forms
This self will not leave blood on boulders
For it has no color, yet to kill it would be sinful
I stay quiet, hide my traces, yet I tear at night's curtain
With my damped-down eyes, secretive like hearts of stones
A lone soul can perhaps hear the earth's heartbeat
But I like best to gaze at stars in the sky
Forgetting how long, until tears stream from my eyes

13

A deadly bullet was fired
At my brother, the snow leopard named White Silver
The gunman just crooked his finger
And echoes of a grim trumpet
Spread news of death through the valley
That bullet was fired

我们灵敏的眼睛,短暂地失忆
虽然看见了它,像一道红色的闪电
刺穿了焚烧着的时间和距离
但已经来不及躲藏
黎明停止了喘息
就是那颗子弹
它的发射者的头颅,以及
为这个头颅供给血液的心脏
已经被罪恶的账簿冻结
就是那颗子弹,像一滴血
就在它穿透目标的那一个瞬间
射杀者也将被眼前的景象震撼
在子弹飞过的地方
群山的哭泣发出伤口的声音
赤狐的悲鸣再没有停止
岩石上流淌着晶莹的泪水
蒿草吹响了死亡的笛子
冰河在不该碎裂的时候开始巨响
天空出现了地狱的颜色
恐惧的雷声滚动在黑暗的天际
我们的每一次死亡,都是生命的控诉!

14

你问我为什么坐在石岩上哭?
无端地哭,毫无理由地哭
其实,我是想从一个词的反面
去照亮另一个词,因为此时

But our keen eyes had a lapse
Although we saw it
Like a streak of red lightning
There was no time to take cover
As hot fire pierced time and distance
And those deep breaths at dawn were extinguished
The bullet was fired, and so
The gunman's skull and the heart
That supplied his skull with blood
Are now frozen forever within annals of sin
Because of that bloody bullet
At the instant it pierced its target
The gunman would be shaken by the sight
And where the bullet flew
Sobbing mountains make a wounded sound
The red fox's keening continues up to now
Crystalline teardrops trickle on boulders
Wormwood blows the flute- song of death
A buckling glacier booms out of season
Colors of hell appear in the sky
Thunder of dread rolls at the dark skyline
With each of our deaths, life brings an indictment!

14

You ask why I sit upon a crag crying
Why that crying mood came over me for no reason
In fact I wish, from the reverse side of a word
To illuminate another word, because in this phase

它正置身于泪水充盈的黑暗

我要把埋在石岩阴影里的头

从雾的深处抬起，用一双疑惑的眼睛

机警地审视危机四伏的世界

所有生存的方式，都来自于祖先的传承

在这里古老的太阳，给了我们温暖

伸手就能触摸的，是低垂的月亮

同样是它们，用一种宽厚的仁慈

让我们学会了万物的语言，通灵的技艺

是的，我们渐渐地已经知道

这个世界亘古就有的自然法则

开始被人类一天天地改变

钢铁的声音，以及摩天大楼的倒影

在这个地球绿色的肺叶上

留下了血淋淋的伤口，我们还能看见

就在每一分钟的时空里

都有着动物和植物的灭绝在发生

我们知道，时间已经不多

无论是对于人类，还是对于我们自己

或许这已经就是最后的机会

因为这个地球全部生命的延续，已经证实

任何一种动物和植物的消亡

都是我们共同的灾难和梦魇

在这里，我想告诉人类

我们大家都已无路可逃，这也是

你看见我只身坐在岩石上

失声痛哭的原因！

That word is situated in tearful darkness

This head of mine, buried in shadows of boulders—

Let me raise it out of fog, and with questioning eyes

Scrutinize the lurking dangers of our world

Our ways of surviving came down from our forefathers

The immemorial sun provides us with warmth

Within closer reach are those low- hanging moons

They too show kindness through the seasons and help us

To heed the language of all things, to commune with spirits

Indeed it has come to our knowledge

That nature's timeless laws over this world

Are being altered every day by mankind

Clang of steel and shadow of high rises

On the green lungs of this planet

Have left bloody wounds, and we can see

With every passing year

Extinction of creatures is happening

We know there is not much time left

Not for humankind, not for ourselves

Maybe this is already our last chance

Because the course of all life on earth attests

To let any kind of plant or animal fade away

Would threaten disaster for all in common

Here is what I would wish to tell human beings

There is no escape route for any of us

This is why you see me here alone

Sitting on a crag, racked by sobs!

15

我是另一种存在,常常看不见自己
除了在灰色的岩石上重返
最喜爱的还是,繁星点点的夜空
因为这无限的天际
像我美丽的身躯,幻化成的图案

为了证实自己的发现
轻轻地呼吸,我会从一千里之外
闻到草原花草的香甜
还能在瞬间,分辨出羚羊消失的方位
甚至有时候,能够准确预测
是谁的蹄印,落在了山涧的底部

我能听见微尘的声音
在它的核心,有巨石碎裂
还有若隐若现的银河
永不复返地熄灭
那千万个深不见底的黑洞
闪耀着未知的白昼

我能在睡梦中,进入濒临死亡的状态
那时候能看见,转世前的模样
为了减轻沉重的罪孽,我也曾经
把赎罪的钟声敲响

15

I am a curious kind of being, often unable to see myself
Unless I get back among these dun- colored crags
Most of all I like the night sky thick with stars
Because the sky's boundless reaches
Look like this lovely coat, these designs spun from the void

To confirm my own discovery
I sniff the air and catch a scent
Of sweet grassland flowers hundreds of miles away
In a wink I can detect where an antelope took cover
At times I can accurately foresee
Whose hoof will alight at the bottom of that ravine

I can hear the sound of a dust mote
At its core was a giant rock that split
And further in a galaxy, barely an inkling
Now irrevocably extinguished
And the bottomless depths of countless black holes
Holding muted refulgence of yet unknown daybreaks

In dreamy sleep, I enter a near- death state
There I see my pre- incarnated form
To lighten the heavy load of sin, I too
Once rang the bells of redemption

虽然我有九条命，但死亡的来临
也将同来世的新生一样正常……

16

我不会写文字的诗
但我仍然会——用自己的脚趾
在这白雪皑皑的素笺上
为未来的子孙，留下
自己最后的遗言

我的一生，就如同我们所有的
先辈和前贤一样，熟悉并了解
雪域世界的一切，在这里
黎明的曙光，比黄昏的落日
还要诱人，那完全是
因为白雪反光的作用
不是在每一个季节，我们都能
享受幸福的时光
或许，这就是命运和生活的无常
有时还会为获取生存的食物
被尖利的碎石划伤
但尽管如此，我欢乐的日子
还是要比悲伤的时日更多

我曾看见过许多壮丽的景象
可以说，是这个世界别的动物

Despite my nine lives, death's coming will be

A matter of course, just like my new life in the world to come...

16

I cannot compose poems in writing

Yet I am able—using my own paws

On unruled stationery of glittery snow

To leave my last will and testament

For sons and grandsons to come

Like my admired forefathers

It has taken me a lifetime to learn

All I need to understand of this snowy region

Here the glow of coming dawn

Due to reflectivity of snow

Is more enticing than dusky sunset

Blessed times may not be ours to enjoy

In every month of every season

Such is the impermanence of life and fate

Sometimes to catch food for survival

We receive cuts from sharp- edged stones

Even so our joyful days

Outnumber our days of sorrow

I have seen so many grand views

It is safe to say, no other animal in the world

当然也包括人类，闻所未闻
不是因为我的欲望所获
而是伟大的造物主对我的厚爱
在这雪山的最高处，我看见过
液态的时间，在蓝雪的光辉里消失
灿烂的星群，倾泻出芬芳的甘露
有一束光，那来自宇宙的纤维
是如何渐渐地落入了永恒的黑暗

是的，我还要告诉你一个秘密
我没有看见过地狱完整的模样
但我却找到了通往天堂的入口！

17

这不是道别
原谅我！我永远不会离开这里
尽管这是最后的领地
我将离群索居，在人迹罕至的地方

不要再追杀我，我也是这个
星球世界，与你们的骨血
连在一起的同胞兄弟
让我在黑色的翅膀笼罩之前
忘记虐杀带来的恐惧

当我从祖先千年的记忆中醒来
神授的语言，将把我的双唇

Not even humans of course, could conceive of them
Such views were not gained by my own desire
But through generosity of the great creator
On the heights of these snowy mountains I have seen
Time in a liquid state, gathered into blue- tinged snowpack
Splendid star- fields that emanate bracing scents of dew
And how light beams, starting from the very fibers of the cosmos
Will eventually fall into eternal darkness

Indeed, I am here to tell you my secret
I have not seen Hell in any coherent shape
But I found an entranceway leading to Heaven!

17

This is not a farewell
Bear with me! Never will I leave this final territory
Though I have been pushed back many times
I will go off and live alone, where human traces seldom come

Do not hunt me down
Here on this planetary world, for I am your brother
Connected to you by blood and bone
Before dark wings come to envelop me
Let me forget the terror of slaughter

In my forefathers' long fund of memory, as I myself awake
Spirit- given language makes my lips into ritual vessels

变成道具，那父子连名的传统
在今天，已成为反对一切强权的武器

原谅我！我不需要廉价的同情
我的历史、价值体系以及独特的生活方式
是我在这个大千世界里
立足的根本所在，谁也不能代替！

不要把我的图片放在
众人都能看见的地方
我害怕，那些以保护的名义
对我进行的看不见的追逐和同化！

原谅我！这不是道别
但是我相信，那最后的审判
绝不会遥遥无期！

①乔治·夏勒（1933—　），美国动物学家、博物学家、自然保护主义者和作家。他曾被美国《时代周刊》评为世界上三位最杰出的野生动物研究学者之一，也是世界公认的最杰出的雪豹研究专家。

And my name linked to my father's name
Now becomes a weapon against naked power!

Bear with me! I need no facile sympathy
My history and way of life, by my own values,
Is what I stand by
In this world of worlds, brooking no substitute!

Do not display my picture
In places where the crowd can see it
I fear their pursuit…their attempts to assimilate me
All done in the name of protection

Bear with me! This is not a farewell
But I believe: The time until final judgment
Will not be dragged out endlessly…!

①*George Beals Schaller, born 1933, is an American zoologist, naturalist, conservationist and author. He was rated by Time magazine as one of the world's leading wildlife researchers. His outstanding work studying and developing conservation initiatives for the snow leopard is acknowledged worldwide.*

致马雅可夫斯基[1]

> 艺术作品始终像它应该的那样,在后世得到复活,穿过拒绝接受它的若干时代的死亡地带。 ——亚·勃洛克[2]

正如你预言的那样,凛冽的风吹着
你的铜像被竖立在街心的广场
人们来来去去,生和死每天都在发生
虽然已经有好长的时间,那些——
曾经狂热地爱过你的人,他们的子孙
却在灯红酒绿中渐渐地把你放在了
积满尘土的脑后,纵然在那雕塑的
阴影里,再看不到痨病鬼咳出的痰
也未见——娼妓在和年轻的流氓厮混
但是,在那高耸入云的电子广告牌下
毒品贩子们和阴险的股市操纵者
却把人类绝望的面孔反射在墙面
从低处看上去,你那青铜岩石的脸部
每一块肌肉的块面都保持着自信
坚定深邃的目光仍然朝着自己的前方
总有人会在你的身边驻足——
那些对明天充满着不安而迷惘的悲观者
那些在生活中还渴望找到希望的人
他们都试图在你脸上,找到他们的答案
这也许就是你的价值,也是你必须要
活下去的理由,虽然他们不可能

For Vladimir Mayakovsky[①]

A true work of art will be resurrected at the proper time, after passing through the deathly hiatus of an era that refuses it. —*Alexander Blok*[②]

As you foretold, your bronze statue's erected
In a crossroads plaza where icy winds blow;
People pass by; some are born and some die.
The ones who were love- struck for your sake
Are long gone, and their descendants,
Booze- fueled under flashy lights, now place you
In dusty oblivion. Now in your statue's shadow
No TB sufferer can be seen spitting up phlegm,
No young hoodlum flitting through a brothel door;
Yet under a LED signboard, against the skyline,
Drug pushers and inside traders still make us see
The blank face of human despair on a wall's surface.
To one looking upwards at your face in craggy bronze,
Each muscular segment as confident as ever,
Your steady gaze still pierces the space ahead.
There will always be some who pause beside you,
Lost souls trembling at thoughts of tomorrow
Or people who search for hope all through life.
At some point they look for answers in your face:
This is perhaps your value, and this is why
You must go on living, though none can see

在你的额头上看到你所遭受过的屈辱
以及你为了自己的信念所忍受的打击
因为你始终相信——你会有复活的那一天
那一个属于你的光荣的时刻——
必将在未来新世纪的一天轰然来临!

你应该回来了,可以用任何一种
方式回来,因为我们早就认识你
你用不着再穿上——那件黄色的
人们熟悉的短衬衫。你就是你!
你可以从天空回来,云的裤子
不是每一个未来主义者的标志,我知道
你不是格瓦拉③,更不是桑迪诺④
那些独裁者和银行家最容易遗忘你
因为你是一个彻头彻尾的诗人
你回来——不是革命的舞蹈者的倒立
而是被命运再次垂青的马蹄铁
你可以从城市的任何一个角落
影子一般回来,因为你嘴唇的石斧
划过光亮的街石,每一扇窗户
都会发出久违了的震耳欲聋的声响

你是词语粗野的第一个匈奴
只有你能吹响断裂的脊柱横笛
谁说在一个战争与革命的时代
除了算命者,就不会有真的预言大师
它不是轮盘赌,唯有你尖利的法器
可刺穿光明与黑暗的棋盘,并能在
琴弦的星座之上,看见羊骨的谜底
一双琥珀的大手,伸进风暴的杯底

What affronts your proud brow endured,
What blows you suffered for your beliefs.
You trusted in your day of resurrection,
Believed the moment of glory you deserved
Would surely come about in the new century!

It's high time you returned; any way you return
Would be fine—now that we recognize you
No need to put on that yellow waistcoat
People knew you by. Who else could you be?
Just come straight from the sky: a cloud in trousers
Isn't the trademark of a run-of-the-mill futurist
Admittedly, not being Che Guevara[3] or Augusto Sandino[4],
You'll hardly register in minds of dictators and bankers
Because you're a thorough poet from head to toe;
By inversion [of soul] you'll return, not on revolution's dance floor
But to the rhythm of hoofbeats, by fate's renewed favor
You'll return on any corner of the city,
Shadowlike—yet the air will split thunderously
Again, at windows over bright paving stones
That you quarried with the adze of your lips,

You—first of all Huns to go on a rampage in language
Only you can coax notes from a broken backbone flute.
An era of war and revolution had its fortune tellers
But who's to say it had no master of prophecy?
It wasn't a roulette game; only your thunderbolt scepter
Could penetrate the chessboard of murkiness and light
Solving sheep-bone riddles by the star signs of lyre strings.
Hermetic barrel-throat, with the yank of a magnetic bridle bit

隐遁的粗舌，抖紧了磁石的马勒
那是婴儿临盆的喊叫，是上帝在把
门铃按响——开启了命运的旅程！

也许你就是刚刚到来的那一个使徒
伟大的祭司——你独自戴着荆冠
你预言的1916就比1917相差了一年
这个世界的巨石发出了滚动前的吼声
那些无知者曾讥笑过你的举动
甚至还打算把你钉上谎言的十字架
他们哪里知道——是你站在高塔上
看见了就要来临的新世纪的火焰
直到今天——也不是所有的人
都知道你宝贵的价值，那些芸芸众生
都认为你已经死亡，只属于过去
但是——这当然不是事实，因为
总有人会得出与大多数不同的结论
那个或许能与你比肩的女人——
茨维塔耶娃[5]就曾说过："力量——在那边！"
毫无疑问，这是一个旷世的天才
对另一个同类最无私的肯定
但是为了这一句话，她付出了代价
她曾把你俩比喻成快腿的人
在你死后，她还公开朗读你的诗作
并为你写下了《高于十字架和烟囱……》
1932年那篇有关你诗歌精妙的文字
赞颂了你在俄罗斯诗歌史上的地位
如今你们两个人都生活在自己
命名的第三个国度，那里既不是天堂
也不是地狱，而作为人在生前

Releasing a newborn infant's cry, none other than the Lord
Ringing a doorbell—commencing fate's next journey,

Perhaps you're the most newly arrived apostle,
Esteemed priest, wearing your personal crown of thorns
You foretold the year 1916, just one year off from 1917
The world's megalith roared out before its careening roll,
But the ignorant jeered at your actions
Laid plans to nail you onto a cross of lies.
How could they know you stood atop a tower
And saw the flames of the new century?
Even up to now, not everyone can know
Your precious value; many in the moiling crowd
Suppose you've died and belong to the past
But of course this isn't true, for some will reach
A conclusion quite unlike the majority's view:
Take that woman who's perhaps on a par with you—
Tvetaeva[5], who once said, "The power...is with him!" —
Was herself a talent rare in any age;
She declared you were one of her kind
Yet she paid a price for making that statement.
She once likened the two of you to fleet runners;
After your death, she recited your poems in public
And wrote "Smokestack Taller than the Cross,"
An essay in tribute to your gifts as a poet
Affirming your rank in the history of Russian poetry,
And now you both live in a realm of your own naming
Which is neither heaven nor hell
Though during your days on this earth

都是用相近的方式,杀死了——自己!
也只有你们,被自发的力量主宰
才能像自己得出的结论那样:
像人一样活着,像诗人一样死去!

不知道是在昨天,还是在比昨天
更糟糕的前一天,你未来的喉咙
被时间的当铺抵押,尽管放出的是高利贷
但你预言性的诗句还是比鲜血更红
这是光阴的深渊,这个跨度令人胆寒
不是所有的精神和思想都能飞越
为你喝彩,没有牙齿的剃了光头的巨人
你已经再一次翻过了时间的尸体
又一次站在了属于你的灯塔的高处
如果不是无知的偏见和卑劣的质疑
没有人真的敢去否认你的宏大和广阔
你就是语言世界的——又一个酋长

是你在语言的铁毡上挂满金属的宝石
呼啸的阶梯,词根的电流闪动光芒
是你又一次创造了前所未有的形式
掀开了棺木上的石板,让橡木的脚飞翔
因为你,俄罗斯古老纯洁的语言
才会让大地因为感动和悲伤而战栗
那是词语的子弹——它钻石般的颅骨
被你在致命的庆典时施以魔法
因为你,形式在某种唯一的时刻
才能取得没有悬念的最后的引力
当然,更是因为你——诗歌从此
不仅仅只代表一个人,它要为——

Both of you—in similar ways—cut your own lives short!
And only you two, ruled by autonomous powers
Could arrive at the conclusion you did:
Live like a human being; die like a poet!

Was it yesterday, or was it the even- more wretched day
Before that, when your throat that belongs to the future,
Was pledged in time's pawnshop, held at a usurious rate?
Yet your oracle brighter than red blood is still undulled
On the far side of time's abyss, cut off by a frightful span
Not to be leaped over by a common power of thought.
Hearing my hurrahs, O toothless, shaven- headed giant.
Again we see you cresting time's moribund slope
Once more to claim your beacon's proper height!
What voice but one of prejudice and resentment
Would dare to deny your heart's vast amplitude?
You stand as a chieftain—in the world of language

Decking concertina wire with powerfully glinting jewels
On a howling stair flashing with high- voltage word roots.
You were the creator of forms that never existed,
You lifted crypt lids, baring oak planks to flight paths in air;
Because of you the pure ancient Russian tongue
Caused the good earth to tremble mournfully;
You fired word- bullets, casting spells with abandon,
Emitted every last scintilla from your diamond skull;
You hit upon forms at just the right moment
And resolved them into inevitable gravity;
In your hands, of course, a poem would convey more
Than the concerns of one mere man, for it would become

更多的人祈求同情、怜悯和保护
无产者的声音和母亲悄声的哭泣
才有可能不会被异化的浪潮淹没
我知道，你也并非是一个完人偶像
道德上的缺陷，从每个凡人身上都能找到
那些关于你的流言蜚语和无端中伤
哪怕是诅咒——也无法去改变
今天的造访者对你的热爱和尊敬
原谅这个世纪！我的马雅可夫斯基
你已经被他们——形形色色追逐名利的
那一群，用各种理由遮蔽得太久
就在昨天，他们看见你的光芒势不可当
他们还试图将一个完整的你分割
——"这一块是未来主义"
——"那一块是社会主义"
他们一直想证明，你创造过奇迹
但在最后的时光，虽然你还活着
你却已经在十年前的那个下午死去
他们无数次地拿出你的遗书——
喋喋不休，讥讽一个死者的交代
他们并不是不知道，你的小舟
已经在大海的深处被撞得粉碎
的确正如你所言——在这种生活里
死去并不困难，但是把生活弄好
却要困难得多！然而天才总是不幸的
在他们生活的周围总会有垃圾和苍蝇
这些鼠目寸光之徒，只能近视地看见
你高筒皮靴上的污泥、斑点和油垢

马雅可夫斯基，黎明时把红色

A plea of sympathy and succor for many.
Cries of landless toilers and sobs of mothers
Were spared from being engulfed in alienation's tide.
I know, you were far from being a perfect idol,
Like any mortal, you had faults and foibles,
But none of the foul rumors and slurs on your name—
None of the curses—can detract from the warm love
Of admirers who are coming to pay respects today.
Forgive the denizens of this century! O Mayakovsky,
For too long they have rendered you invisible,
All those who slaver and jostle after fame and profit;
Even now your brilliance is too much for them
They attempt to break apart your wholeness:
— "This piece of him is futurist"
— "This piece of him is socialist"
In spite of your miraculous production
They try to prove that in waning years
Your life dragged out without creative fire,
Repeatedly trotting out your last testament,
Holding up a dying man's instructions to ridicule.
They must have known that perilous waves
Had staved in the sides of your lifeboat by then,
Just as you said—it isn't difficult to die
In this life; the difficult thing is to live well.
Yet a genius must always taste misery
And be pestered by garbage- swarming flies;
Members of the rat- eyed breed were only fit
To peer at mud and grease spots on your jackboots.

Mayakovsky, house- painter applying swaths of red

抹上天幕的油漆工,你天梯的骨肋
伸展内核的几何,数字野兽的支架
打破生物学方案闪电脚后的幻变
面颊通过相反吞噬渴望的现代板凳
没有返回的刀鞘,被加减的迟速
三倍吹响十月没有局部完全的整体
属于立体飓风的帆,只有腹部的镰刀
被粗糙定型的生物才有孕育的资格
马雅可夫斯基,没有一支铠甲的武装
能像你一样,在语言的边界,发动了
一场比核能量更有威力的进攻
难怪有人说,在那个属于你的诗的国度
你的目光也能把冰冷的石头点燃
他们担心你还会把传统从轮船上扔下
其实你对传统的捍卫,要比那些纯粹的
形式主义者们坚定百倍
你孩童般的狡黠帮助你战胜了争吵
对传统的冒犯——你这个家伙,从来
就是用以吸引大众目光的一种策略
马雅可夫斯基,不用其他人再给你评判
你就是那个年代——诗歌大厅里
穿着粗呢大衣的独一无二的中心
不会有人忘记——革命和先锋的结合
是近一百年所有艺术的另一个特征
它所产生的影响是巨大的,就是在
反越战的时候,艾伦·金斯伯格[6]们
在纽约的街头嚎叫,但在口袋里装着的
却是你炙手可热的滚烫的诗集

你的诗,绝不是纺毛的喑哑的羊羔

To heaven's vault at dawn, your ribs like heaven's ladder
Unfolded geometry from the core, frame of numerical beast
With counter-biological schemes sparking behind your feet,
Cheeks hollow from swallowed longing, on a modernist bench,
A sheath of no return, slowness tweaked to a speedy edge,
Totality of the incomplete trumpeted through three Octobers,
Sail hoisted in cubist cyclone; sickle blade that's one big belly,
Only a creature formed in rough strife gets to conceive.
Mayakovsky, who could resemble you?
Bare of all armor, from frontiers of language mounting
An attack more awesome than any nuclear blast,
No wonder some call you ruler in the land of poetry
And say your merest glance ignites icy rocks there;
They fear you'll throw tradition overboard, but
In truth, you are tradition's stout upholder
More steadfast by far than any formalist:
Childlike yet blessed with wit to sidestep quarrels,
Sly old fox thumbing your nose at tradition
But only as a strategy to gain an audience,
Mayakovsky, you need no validation from critics.
Poetry in that era could fill auditoriums, and you
In your serge greatcoat occupied the central place.
We recall your bond between revolution and avant-garde
Which was a defining feature of our past century,
Its influence penetrating so many areas,
Even anti-Vietnam War protests, when Ginsberg[6] and friends
Carried your ardent, red-blooded book of poems with them.

Your poetry isn't lamb's wool quietly spun; it surges forward

是涌动在街头奔跑的双刃，坚硬的结构
会让人民恒久的沉默——响彻宇宙
是无家可归者的房间，饥饿打开的门
是大海咬住的空白，天空牛皮的鼓面
你没有为我们布道，每一次巡回朗诵
神授的语言染红手指，喷射出来
阶梯的节奏总是在更高的地方结束
无论是你的低语，还是雷霆般的轰鸣
你的声音都是这个世界上——
为数不多的仅次于神的声音，当然你不是神
作为一个彻底的唯物主义者，你的
一生都在与不同的神进行彻底的抗争
你超自然的朗诵，打动过无数的心灵
与你同时代的听众，对此有过精彩的描述
马雅可夫斯基，我们今天仍然需要你
并不是需要再去重复一段生活和历史
谁也无法否认，那些逝去的日子里
也有杀戮、流亡、迫害和权力的滥用
惊心动魄的改变，谎言被铸造成真理
不是别的动物，而是文明的——人
亲自制造了一幕幕令人发指的悲剧
马雅可夫斯基，尽管这样，人类从未
能打破生和死的规律，该死亡的——
从未停止过死亡，该诞生的每天仍然在诞生
死去的有好人，当然也有恶棍
刚出生的未必都是善良之辈，但是
未来会成为流氓的一定是少数
这个世界最终只能由诚实和善良来统治
马雅可夫斯基，并不是一个偶然的发现
20 世纪和 21 世纪两个世纪的开端

In street actions, and the tempering of its rapier blade
Stops short all marchers up short who hear it clangs through the cosmos.
It's a hostel for the homeless, a door opened by hunger,
Ocean's teeth clamped onto blankness, an ox-hide drumhead of sky.
You never evangelized, yet throughout your reading tours
Divine speech reddened your hands, poured forth in geysers;
Your rhythmic staircase swept us toward the heights
Whether in a whispers or thunderous roars.
Yours was one of few voices on earth that was able
To impart a divine spark to words—with your human throat,
Yet you were a diehard materialist,
All your life opposed to theism in any form.
Your readings had uncanny impact on countless hearts
And audience members raved in contemporary accounts.
We still need you, not to bring back one era of history;
Who can deny the abuses of power during your era?
It was used to kill and banish and persecute people,
It fomented terrible upheavals, printed lies in boldface,
Such hair-raising travesties were committed
Not by other animals, but by civilized humans;
Yet in spite of all their exertions
Nothing but death awaited them:
When it comes time to die or be born
No one can get around the basic rules.
Good people keep on dying, just as evil ones do;
Not all newborns will turn out good-hearted
But future malefactors will surely be in the minority;
After all, only honesty and kindness can rule this world.
Mayakovsky, it wasn't a matter of happenstance
The opening years of both the 20th and the 21st centuries

都有过智者发出这样的喟叹——
道德的沦丧,到了丧心病狂的地步
精神的堕落,更让清醒的人们不安
那些卑微的个体生命——只能
匍匐在通往灵魂被救赎的一条条路上
马雅可夫斯基,并非每一个人都是怀疑论者
在你的宣言中,从不把技术逻辑的进步
——用来衡量人已经达到的高度
你以为第三次精神革命的到来——
已经成了不可阻挡的又一次必然
是的,除了对人的全部的热爱和奉献
这个世界的发展和进步难道还有别的意义?

马雅可夫斯基,礁石撞击的大海
语言中比重最有分量的超级金属
浮现在词语波浪上的一艘巨轮
穿越城市庞大胸腔的蒸汽机车
被堆积在旷野上的文字的巨石阵
撕破油布和马鞍的疯狂的呓语
难以诉诸孤独野牛鲜红的壮硕

马雅可夫斯基,这哪里是你的全部
你的追随者也曾希望,能在你的诗歌里
尝到爱人舌尖上——滴下的蜜
其实,他们只要去读一读你写给
勃里克[7]的那些柔美的信和野性的诗
就会知道哪怕你写情诗,你也一定是
那个领域里不可多得的高手,否则
你也不会给雅可夫列娃[8]留下这样的诗句:
"她爱?她不爱?我只能扼腕

Were greeted by heavy sighs from our wisest thinkers
Over moral decline that resulted in acts of depravity;
They could feel a worrisome ebbing of the human spirit;
What would be left for beings laid low and isolated
But for each to crawl to redemption along its own road?
Mayakovsky, not everyone's a skeptic like yourself;
Your manifestos never treated questions of pure logic
As a measure of advancement in human character.
You believed a third spiritual revolution was imminent
Like earlier stages, its necessity wasn't to be obstructed,
Yet aside from selfless service and the fulfillment of love
The world's so- called progress would hold little meaning.

Mayakovsky—great shoal exposed to battering of waves
With language so rich in metal you mined,
Great steamship cruising over the ocean of letters,
Locomotive passing through the city's huge chest,
Stonehenge of written words on a broad, open plain,
Babble of manic wind tearing at tarpaulins and saddles,
Wild crimson bull, asserting massive strength in solitude;

Mayakovsky, all this is far from your totality.
Your followers also sought out your poems
To taste the honey that drips from a lover's lips.
We need only read what you sent to Lilya Brik[7]
All those tender, stormy love notes and verses
To learn of your rare gifts in that domain as well.
How else could you have penned these lines to Yakovleva[8]?
"She loves me, she loves me not...be still my hand!

我不顾这碎片去极力猜测——
五月却迎来了送葬的甘菊"
但是，不！这不是你，更不是你的命运
早已经为你做出了义无反顾的决定
你的诗将永远不是小猫发出的呷鸣之声
你从一开始注定就是词语王国里的大力士
当然，你不是唯一的独角兽，与你为伍的
还有巴波罗·聂鲁达[9]、巴列霍[10]、阿蒂拉[11]、
奈兹瓦尔[12]、希克梅特[13]、布罗涅夫斯基[14]
不能被遗忘的扬尼斯·里索斯[15]、帕索里尼[16]
他们都是你忠诚的同志和亲如手足的兄弟
马雅可夫斯基，这些伟大的心灵尊重你
是因为你——在劳苦大众集会的广场上
掏出过自己红色的心——展示给不幸的人们
你让真理的手臂返回，并去握紧劳动者的手
因此，诗人路易·阿拉贡[17]深情地写道：
"革命浪尖上的诗人，是他教会了我
如何面对广大的群众，面对新世界的建设者
这个以诗为武器的人改变了我的一生"
不是唱过赞歌的人，都充满了真诚
然而，对你的真诚，我们从未有过怀疑
与那些投机者相比较，你的彷徨和犹豫
——也要比他们更要可爱和纯粹！
那些没有通过心脏和肺叶的所谓纯诗
还在评论家的书中被误会拔高，他们披着
乐师的外袍，正以不朽者的面目穿过厅堂
他们没有竖琴，没有动人的嘴唇
只想通过语言的游戏而获得廉价的荣耀
诚然，对一个诗人而言，马雅可夫斯基
不是你所有的文字都能成为经典

Lay by these restless surmises in fallen petals
Yet May greets me with chrysanthemum funeral wreaths!"
But you wouldn't be held to this—the fate of a lover;
Early on you were steeled in your resolve
Never to let your poems be a tomcat's howls;
You were born to be a stalwart in the realm of letters
But not its sole unicorn; by your side stood others
Such as Neruda[9] and Vallejo[10] and Joszef[11]
With Nezval[12] and Hikmet[13] and Broniewski[14]
And who could forget Ritsos[15] and Pasolini[16]?
All were your faithful comrades, brothers in all but flesh.
Mayakovsky, these great souls paid honor to you
Because you bared your heart before unfortunate souls
On public squares where the laboring masses gathered,
Your hand reclaiming truth by clasping their calloused hands,
Which is why Louis Aragon[17] poured out these lines:
"Poet on the wave-crest of revolution, he taught me
To face the broad masses, to face the builders of our world!"
Not all praise singers turn out to be sincere in the end
But for us your sincerity's never been in doubt;
Compared to opportunists, even in your dithering moments
You exerted a certain appeal, because of your purity.
As for "pure poems" not summoned from heart and guts,
Some critics mistakenly puff them in books, and such poets
Are feted in maestros' robes for works of "enduring value"
Yet they possess no lyre, no lips that touch people's hearts:
They intend to gain glory cheaply with their language games.
In truth, Mayakovsky, speaking poet to poet,
Not all your writings can become classics:

你也有过教条、无味，甚至太直接的表达
但是，毫无疑问——可以肯定！
你仍然是那个时代最伟大的诗的公民
而那些用文字沽名钓誉者，他们最多
只能算是——小圈子里自大的首领！
当然，他们更不会是诗歌疆域里的雄狮
如果非要给他们命名——
他们顶多是贵妇怀中慵懒的宠物
否则，在你死的时候，你长脸的兄长
帕斯捷尔纳克[⑱]，就不会为你写出动人的诗篇
你的突入，比所有的事物都要夺目
在你活着的时候，谁也无法快过你的速度
你最终跨进传说只用了一步，以死亡的方式！

你从不服从于油腻溢满思想的君王
从一开始，你的愤世嫉俗，不可一世
就让那些无知者认为——你仅仅是一个
不足挂齿的没有修养的狂妄之徒
而那些因为你的革命和先锋的姿态
来对你的诗句和人生做狭隘判断的人
他们在乌烟瘴气的沙龙里——
一直在传播着诋毁你的逸言和轶事
用这样的方式，他们已经不是一次两次
埋葬了诗的头盖骨，这是惯用的伎俩
他们——就曾经把你亲密的兄弟和对手
叶赛宁[⑲]说成是一个醉汉和好色之徒
实际上你知道——他是俄罗斯田园
最后一位用眼泪和心灵悲戚的歌者
叶赛宁的死，就如同你的死一样
从未让任何个人和集团在道义上负责

You wrote dogmatic, insipid, prosaic passages as well,
Yet without a doubt it must be affirmed
You were that era's greatest poet-citizen!
As for those who fish in words for the bubble reputation,
They'll amount to no more than leaders of coteries.
How could they ever be lions on the savannas of poetry?
If I'm asked to liken them to something
I can only see them as lap-dogs for rich ladies,
But you, my brother of the long face, were of such stuff
That a man like Pasternak[⑱] wrote a moving tribute in verse.
Your leaps are more captivating than any literal object;
While you were alive, no one could match your speed.
You lived one step from legend, with death your means of entry.

You never submitted to rulers born to eat from silver spoons:
From the start your contempt for convention, your haughtiness
Guaranteed that the ignorant would slap a label on you
As an uncultivated maniac, unworthy of mention
And those chatterers holding forth in miasmic salons
Who judged your life and poems by narrow standards
Because of your revolutionary, avant-garde stance
Were quick to circulate slurs and demeaning anecdotes.
Again and again they resorted to such means—
Up to their usual tricks—burying the cranium of poetry underfoot;
In such a way they treated Yesenin[⑲], your beloved friend and rival
Whom they claimed to be a drunk and a sex fiend,
But you know—he poured out heart and tears
To sing the final elegies for pastoral life in Russia;
Yet after Yesenin's death, as after yours
No person or group discharged their moral duty.

我不知道传统的东正教的俄罗斯
是什么模样？但从他忧郁的诗句里
我可以听到——吟诵死亡的斯拉夫民歌
在断裂的树皮上流下松脂一般的眼泪

马雅可夫斯基，因为你相信人的力量
才从未在上帝和神的面前下跪
你编织的语言，装饰彗星绽放的服饰
那永不衰竭的喉管，抽搐的铆钉
你的诗才是这个世界一干二净的盐
如果有一种接骨木，能让灵魂出窍
那是刻骨铭心的愤怒的十二之后
你是胜利者王冠上剧毒反向的块结
因为只有这样——或者相反
才会让你刀削一般高傲的脸庞
在曙光之中被染成太阳古老的黄色
马雅可夫斯基——光明的歌者和黑暗的
宿敌，宣布你已经死亡的人
其实早已全部死亡，他们——
连一些残骸也没有真的留下
当你站在最高的地方——背靠虚脱的云霓
你将目睹人类的列车，如何
驶过惊慌失措，拥挤不堪的城市
那里钢铁发锈的声音，把婴儿的
啼哭压扁成家具，摩天大楼的影子
刺伤了失去家园的肮脏的难民
你能看见——古老的文明在喘息着
这个地球上大部分的土地——
早已被财富的垄断者和奸商们污染
战争还在继续，在逃亡中死去的生命
并不比两次大战的亡灵更少

I don't know how such matters are dealt with
In the Eastern Orthodox faith, but in Yesenin's lines
I hear a threnody in the mode of a Slavic folk song,
See tears of resin where a tree's bark was girdled.

Mayakovsky, you believed in human strength
So you'd never knelt to God or any deity;
You adorned your word- weavings with comet tails,
O never faltering organ pipe, making brackets shudder,
Sharing out- and- out salt of the earth in your poems.
If bones are healed by elder flowers and sent on astral flights,
First let those bones be etched by rage of your twelve furies!
Your victor's crown flaunts carbuncles of poison turned outward
Because only thus, or by means of an even greater extremity,
Can your haughty features carved by knives
Let themselves be dyed golden in mellow light of morning,
Mayakovsky, singer of light and sworn enemy of darkness!
As for those who proclaimed your death
Not even their mortal remains can be found;
As you stand on high, leaning on a rosy cloud bank
You'll look down as mankind's passenger train
Passes through a city full of milling, panicky crowds.
To rust- belt rhythms, outcries of children are being flattened
Into home fixtures, and hulks of high- rise buildings
Jut into the living space of migrants, leaving them in dirt.
You'll see ancient cultures gasping for breath
While a large portion of this planet's land
Is enclosed by capital, polluted by sharp dealers.
War continues, and lives lost in flight from broken states
Will soon rival the number of deaths from both World Wars.

马雅可夫斯基,纵然你能看见飞行器
缩短了火星与人类的距离
可是近在咫尺的灵性,却被物化的
电流击穿,精神沦落为破损的钱币
被割裂的自然,只剩下失血的身体
那些在大地上伫立的冥想和传统
没有最后的归宿——只有贪婪的欲望
在机器的齿轮中,逆向的呐喊声嘶力竭
异化的焦虑迷失于物质的逻辑
这无论是在东方还是西方——
都没有逃脱价值跌落可怕的结局
因为,现实所发生的一切已经证明
那些启蒙者承诺的文本和宣言
如今都变成了舞台上的道具
用伸张正义以及人道的名义进行的屠杀
——从来就没有过半分钟的间歇
他们绑架舆论,妖魔化别人的存在
让强权和武力披上道德的外衣
一批批离乡背井流离失所的游子
只有故土的星星才能在梦中浮现
把所谓文明的制度加害给邻居
这要比哥伦布发现新大陆更要无耻
这个世界可以让航天飞机安全返航
却很难找到一个评判公理的地方
所谓国际法就是一张没有内容的纸
他们明明看见恐怖主义肆意蔓延
却因为自己的利益持完全不同的标准
他们打破了一千个部落构成的国家
他们想用自己的方式代替别人的方式
他们妄图用一种颜色覆盖所有的颜色

Mayakovsky, though you'll see spaceships being built
That put Mars within the reach of humankind,
Souls within a few steps of us are being jolted
By material impulses, pinning aspirations to worn coins.
The natural world's cut apart, leaving its anemic body;
Our contemplative traditions with feet planted on earth
Now have no refuge from the panderers of desire,
Their cries hoarsening against the din of gear-teeth,
Angst turning to another thing, lost in logic of materiality,
And neither Occident nor Orient can find an escape
From the fearsome endgame of collapsing values
As events in the real world are proving all too well:
Texts and proclamations of the "Enlightenment project"
Have by now been turned into stage props
For men who slaughter in the name of justice and humanity
And this has gone on without respite, not even for a minute.
They hijack public opinion; they demonize other people's existence,
They dress autocracy and armed might in moral garments
And inflict a so-called "civilized system" upon one's neighbors,
More shamelessly than Columbus "discovering" the New World.
In this world a space shuttle can be brought back to land safely
But where can we find a place to render a fair judgment?
As for international law, it is a piece of paper empty of content,
Its would-be arbiters watch international terrorism running rampant,
Then interpret "law" in wildly different ways to serve their interests;
They cobble together nation states by breaking up a thousand tribes;
Using their own mode, they expect to replace the modes of others.
They scheme delusively to cover all colors with their own color,

他们让弱势者的文化没有立锥之地
从炎热的非洲到最边远的拉丁美洲
资本打赢了又一场没有硝烟的战争
他们已经大功告成——一种隐形的权力
甚至控制了这个星球不为人知的角落
他们只允许把整齐划一的产品——
说成是所有的种族要活下去的唯一
他们不理解一个手工匠人为何哭泣
他们嘲笑用细竹制成的安第斯山排箫
只因为能够吹奏的人已经寥寥无几
当然，他们无法回答，那悲伤的声音
为什么可以穿越群山和幽深的峡谷
他们摧毁被认定为野蛮人的习惯法
当那些年轻的生命寻求酒精的麻痹
无论是男人还是女人都一样
他们却对旁人说："印第安人就喜欢酒！"
其实，任何一场具有颠覆性的巨变
总有无数的个体生命付出巨大的牺牲
没有别的原因，只有良心的瞭望镜——
才可能在现代化摩天楼的顶部看见
——贫困是一切不幸和犯罪的根源
在21世纪的今天，不用我们举证
那些失去传统、历史以及生活方式的人们
是艾滋病与毒品共同构成的双重的灾难
毫无疑问，这绝不仅仅是个体的不幸
而是整个人类面临的生死存亡的危机
任何对垂危中的生命熟视无睹——
最后的审判都不会被轻易地饶恕

马雅可夫斯基，毫无疑问——
你正穿越一个对你而言陌生的世纪

Grudge even one inch of ground for disadvantaged cultures
From torrid Africa to remote domains of Latin America.
Capital keeps winning its war fought without gunpowder,
Its great "achievement" is assured—its hidden power
Even now exerts control in little-known corners of the globe:
They'll not stop promoting their uniform commodities
Until no other avenues of survival are open to any tribe.
They don't understand the tears of an artisan or craftsman,
They laugh at Andean pan pipes made from thin bamboo
Because hardly anyone can still play them well.
Of course they can't explain that mournful sound,
How it wells up from hidden valleys deep in the mountains;
They ruined native codes of conduct, calling them relics of savagery
And when youngsters took to numbing themselves with alcohol,
They'd tell people, "You see, Indians are fools for liquor."
In fact, when any upheaval comes along and subverts a way of life
The price must be paid in suffering by people who lived that life;
No other telescope but conscience can look from a high-rise rooftop
And see how crime and misery of all kinds are rooted in poverty
Today in the 21st century we need not point out evidence
That peoples deprived of tradition, history and a way of life
Are beset by the twofold disaster of AIDS and drug abuse;
Without a doubt, this is more than misfortune for a certain few,
It's a crisis that threatens the survival of mankind as a whole;
Any callous disregard of humans even now on the verge of death
Won't lightly be forgiven come time for ultimate judgment.

Mayakovsky—there can be no doubt that now
You're venturing into a century quite strange to you,

在这里我要告诉你——我的兄长
你的诗句中其实已经预言过它的凶吉
在通往地狱和天堂的交叉路口上
无神论者、教徒、成千上万肉体的躯壳
他们的心中都有着自己的造物主
当领袖、神父、阿訇、牧师、转世者
以及金钱和国家上层建筑的主导者
把人类编成军队的方阵出发
尽管这样,这个世界为给太阳加温的炉灶
还是在罪行被宽恕前发生了裂变
马雅可夫斯基,时间和生活已经证实
你不朽的诗歌和精神,将凌空而至
飞过死亡的峡谷——一座座无名的高峰
那些无病呻吟的诗人,也将会
在你沉重粗犷的诗句面前羞耻汗颜
你诗歌的星星将布满天幕
那铁皮和银质的诗行会涌入宇宙的字典
你语言的烈士永不会陨落,死而复生
那属于你的未来的纪念碑——
它的构成,不是能被磨损的青铜
更不会是将在腐蚀中风化的大理石
你的纪念碑高大巍峨——谁也无法将它毁灭
因为它的钢筋,将植根于人类精神的底座
马雅可夫斯基,你的语言和诗歌
是大地和海洋所能告知的野蛮的胜利
每一次震动,它的激流都会盖过词语的顶端
或许,这就是你的选择,对于诗的技艺
我知道——从生到死你都在实践并怀着敬意
否则,你就不会去提醒那些匠人
因为他们只注重诗歌的技术和形式
那没有血肉、疼痛、灵性的语言游戏

But here I'd like to tell you, O my brother,
Your poetic lines long ago foretold its bane and blessing;
At the crossroads of heaven and hell, people stand in myriads
As fleshly bodies, and whether they be atheists or believers
Each in his or her own heart carries the creator.
In these times officials, priests, pastors, imams and tulkus
Along with leading figures of finance and state superstructures
Have grouped people in regimented formations to send them forth;
Yet the hearth of this world that could warm the very sun
Is rending at its seams before crimes can be forgiven.
Mayakovsky, the times we lived through offer evidence
Your poetry's immortal spirit is poised to make its advent:
It's flown over a deathly canyon, past nameless peaks.
As for poets who moan before they taste true suffering
Your weighty, hard-hitting lines will shame and chastise them:
The stars of your poem sequences will deck the sky canopy,
Your ironclad, silvery lines will flood into the cosmic lexicon;
Your martyred language is comet-like—no plunging meteor,
The memorial plaque now being erected for you
Won't be made of bronze that can be effaced
And it won't be of marble that can be eroded:
Its reinforcing rods are planted in the human spirit's pedestal;
Mayakovsky, your language and your poems
Are a victory of wildness as told to us by land and sea;
With each impact, words are engulfed to a great depth,
Perhaps by your choice, because throughout life
You practiced the art of poetry as a reverential act,
Otherwise you wouldn't have chided those polishers of prosody
When you saw them devote full attention to technique and form:
Because of word games played without blood and pain and heart

已经让我们的诗开始在战斗中节节败退
马雅可夫斯基，今天不是在占卜的声音中
你才被唤醒，你在此前躺下已经很久
那些善变的政客、伪善的君子、油滑的舌头
他们早就扬言，你的诗歌已进入坟墓
再不会在今天的现实中成为语言的喜马拉雅
但他们哪里知道，你已经越过了忘川
如同燃烧的火焰——已经到了门口
这虽然不是一场你为自己安排的庆典
但你已经到来的消息却被传遍
马雅可夫斯基，这是你的复活——
又一次的诞生，你战胜了沉重的死亡
这不是乌托邦的想象，这就是现实
作为诗人——你的厄运已经结束
那响彻一切世纪的火车，将鸣响汽笛
而你将再一次与我们一道——
用心灵用嘴唇用骨架构筑新的殿堂
成为人的臣仆和思想，而只有冲破了
无尽岁月的诗歌才能用黑夜星星的
贡品——守护肃穆无边的宇宙
并为无数的灵魂在头顶上洒下光辉……

马雅可夫斯基，新的诺亚——
正在曙光照耀的群山之巅，等待
你的方舟降临在陆地和海洋的尽头
诗没有死去，它的呼吸比铅块还要沉重
虽然它不是世界的教士，无法赦免
全部的罪恶，但请相信它始终
会站在人类道德法庭的最高处，一步
也不会离去，它发出的经久不息的声音
将穿越所有的世纪——并成为见证！

Our poetry is starting to lose battles in our common struggle.
Mayakovsky, no diviner made a pronouncement in recent days
To prompt this rousing cry, so long after you laid your body down;
It was the fickleness of politicos, pretending to be sure of themselves
Glibly claiming all these years that your poetry has gone to its grave,
Denying that in today's world it can be a Himalayan peak of language.
Little do they know, you've already crossed the waters of Lethe
Like a seething tongue of flame, and have reached our doorway
Though this isn't a jubilee you arranged for yourself:
News of your arrival is in the air;
Mayakovsky, this is your resurrection, time for a new birth
Having vanquished death's oppressive weight,
This isn't utopian imagination, this is reality.
As a poet, your bitter fate's coming to an end,
That resounding train will whistle down the centuries:
Once again you can pitch in, together with us
And erect a shrine, with heart and lips and anatomy
As servants and thinkers of the people, with time- defying poems,
As offerings that shine like stars through dark nights
For the vigil they keep in the solemn, boundless cosmos
And the light they beam from overhead on countless souls.

Mayakovsky, our new Noah,
By dawn's light, these ranged mountaintops are waiting
For your ark's descent to the ends of land and ocean.
Poetry hasn't died: its breath is heavier than a plumb- line;
Even though it's not the world's priest and can't absolve
The entirety of sins, please believe it will stand
Forever at the height of mankind's moral tribunal
Never taking one step aside, raising its enduring voice
Throughout all the centuries—in acts of testimony!

①马雅可夫斯基（1893—1930），20世纪伟大的俄苏诗人，1930年4月14日自杀，身后留下13卷诗文。

②亚·勃洛克（1880—1921），俄国象征主义流派的领军人物。

③格瓦拉(1928—1967)，生于阿根廷，国际政治家及古巴革命的核心人物。

④桑迪诺（1893—1934），尼加拉瓜民族解放阵线领袖，游击战专家。

⑤茨维塔耶娃（1892—1941），俄苏最著名的诗人之一，也被认为是20世纪俄罗斯最伟大的诗人。

⑥艾伦·金斯伯格（1926—1997），美国著名诗人，被认为是"垮掉的一代"中的领军人物。

⑦勃里克（1891—1978），全名丽莉娅·勃里克，是马雅可夫斯基的同居者、情人。

⑧雅可夫列娃（1906—1991），全名塔吉雅娜·雅可夫列娃，旅居法国的俄裔侨民，马雅可夫斯基曾热烈地追求她。

⑨巴波罗·聂鲁达（1904—1973），生于智利，被誉为20世纪最伟大的拉丁美洲诗人。

⑩巴列霍（1892—1938），20世纪拉丁美洲最有影响的先锋派诗人。

⑪阿蒂拉（1905—1937），20世纪匈牙利最伟大的诗人之一。

⑫奈兹瓦尔（1900—1958），全名维杰斯拉夫·奈兹瓦尔，捷克最具代表性的超现实主义诗人。

⑬希克梅特（1902—1963），全名纳齐姆·希克梅特，20世纪土耳其现代诗歌的奠基者。

⑭布罗涅夫斯基（1897—1962），20世纪波兰著名的革命诗人。

⑮扬尼斯·里索斯（1909—1990），20世纪希腊伟大的革命诗人，希腊现代诗歌的创始人之一。

⑯帕索里尼（1922—1975），20世纪意大利著名诗人、导演，曾参加意大利共产党。

⑰路易·阿拉贡（1897—1982），20世纪法国著名诗人，共产主义者，达达主义和超现实主义的代表性人物之一。

⑱帕斯捷尔纳克（1890—1960），20世纪伟大的俄苏诗人、作家。

⑲叶赛宁（1895—1925），20世纪著名的俄苏诗人，田园派诗歌的代表人物。

①Vladimir Mayakovsky (1893-1930) was a leading Russian modernist poet and playwright. His collected works run to 13 volumes.

②Alexander Aleksandrovich Blok (1880-1921) was the leading figure of Russian symbolist literary movement.

③Che Guevara (1928-1967), born in Argentina, was a leading figure of the revolutionary movement in Cuba and other Latin American countries.

④Augusto Cesar Sandino (1893-1934) was leader of the Nicaraguan liberation movement and leader of its guerilla forces.

⑤Marina Tsvetaeva (1892-1941) was a great poet of the Soviet era.

⑥Allen Ginsberg (1926-1997) was an American poet and core figure of the "Beat Movement."

⑦Lilya Brik (1891-1978) was Mayakovsky's lover and cohabitant.

⑧Tatyana Yakovleva (1906-1991) was a Russian emigre who was wooed in Paris by Mayakovsky.

⑨Pablo Neruda (1904-1973), born in Chile, was the greatest poet of Latin America in the 20th century.

⑩Cesar Vallejo (1892-1938) was an influential avant-garde poet from Latin America.

⑪Atilla Jozsef (1905-1937) was one of Hungary's great 20th century poets.

⑫Vitězslav Nezval (1900-1958) was an outstanding representative of Czechoslovakian surrealist poetry.

⑬Nazim Hikmet (1902-1963) laid the cornerstone for Turkish modern poetry.

⑭Władysław Broniewski (1897-1962) was a famous revolutionary poet of Poland.

⑮Yannis Ristos (1909-1990) was a revolutionary poet and innovator of modern poetry in Greece.

⑯Piero Pasolini (1922-1975) was a famous Italian poet, film director and Communist Party member.

⑰Louis Aragon (1897-1982) was a famous French poet of the Dadaist School and a member of the Communist Party.

⑱Boris Pasternak (1890-1960) was a great 20th century writer and poet in Russian.

⑲Sergei Yesenin (1895-1925) was the outstanding representative of pastoral, lyric poetry in modern Russian.

不朽者

序诗

黑夜里我是北斗七星,
白天又回到了部族的土地。
幸运让我抓住了燃烧的松明,
你看我把生和死都已照亮。

一

我握住了语言的盐,
犹如触电。

二

群山的合唱不是一切。
一把竹质的口弦,
在黑暗中低吟。

三

我没有抓住传统,
在我的身后。

The Enduring One

Proem

By night I am the Big Dipper's seven stars,
By day I return to the soil of my tribe.
By luck I got hold of pitch to burn,
Watch me illuminate life and death with it[①].

1

I grab hold of the salt in language;
It feels like getting an electric shock.

2

Aside from the chorus of ranged mountains,
In the darkness there is a murmur
Of a mouth harp's bamboo reed.

3

I did not grab hold of tradition;
It is behind me. Even extended by shadows

我的身臂不够长,有一截是影子。

四

我无法擦掉,
牛皮碗中的一点污迹。
难怪有人从空中泼下大雨,
在把我冲洗。

五

挂在墙上的宝刀,
突然断裂了。
毕摩①告诉我,他能占卜凶吉,
却不能预言无常。

六

我在口中念诵二的时候,
二并没有变成三;
但我念诵三的时候,
却出现了万物的幻象。

七

昨晚的篝火烧得很旺,
今天却是一堆灰烬,
如果一阵狂风吹过,
不会再有任何墨迹。

My arms were not long enough.

4

In a leather drinking bowl is a smear;
It is hard for me to wipe away;
No wonder someone sends rainfall from the sky
To rinse me clean.

5

A crack suddenly appeared
In the storied sword that hung on the wall.
The bimo[2] says he can divine bane and blessing,
But not the workings of impermanence.

6

As my mouth reads "two" aloud
"Two" does not turn into "three"
But when I read "three" aloud,
Images of a myriad things appear...

7

Last night flames leapt high in the fireplace
Now it is just a heap of ashes.
Even if a tempest blew through
No more ink traces would be stirred today.

八

捡到玛瑙的是一个小孩,
在他放羊的途中。
他不知道自己是一个幸运者,
只梦见得到了一块荞饼。

九

我不是唯一的证人。
但我能听见三星堆②,
在面具的背后,有人发出
咝咝的声音,在叫我的名字。

十

我的身躯,
是火焰最后的一根柴,
如果点燃,你会看见,
它比别的柴火都要亮。

十一

失重的石头。
大雁的影子。
会浮现在歌谣里,像一滴泪
堵住喉头。

8

A chunk of agate was found by a child
As he took his sheep out to pasture
He did not know he was a lucky boy;
He only dreamed of getting a buckwheat cake.

9

I am not the sole witness
But I can hear a sibilant voice,
From a mask found at Sanxing Mound[3],
Someone calling my name.

10

My body is for the flames—
When no other fuel remains;
Once lit you will see its brightness
Like no other piece of firewood.

11

A stone in free- fall,
A distant goose in flight
May show up during a song, like a teardrop
Causing a catch in the throat.

十二

死亡和分娩，
对诗人都是一个奇迹，
因为语言，他被放进了
不朽者的谱系。

十三

火焰灼烫我的时候，
无意识的一声喊叫，
竟然如此陌生。
我不知道，这是我的声音。

十四

那块石头，
我没有从地里捡走。
原谅我，无法确定明日，
我只拥有今天。

十五

我在竹笛和羊角之间。
是神授的语言，
让我咬住了大海的罗盘。

12

Death and parturition—
For the poet, both are a miracle.
Because of language he is given a place
In the lineage of enduring ones.

13

When flames scorch me
The cry that escapes my lips
Sounds quite strange to me;
I cannot be sure it is my voice.

14

I came upon a certain stone
But left it lying in the field.
Forgive me, I cannot be sure of tomorrow;
I only have today.

15

I am between a bamboo flute and a sheep- horn bugle;
God- given language enables my jaws to clamp
Onto a compass made for the vast ocean.

十六

我爬在神的背上,
本想告诉它一个谜。
但是我睡着了,
像一条晨曦中的鲑鱼。

十七

彝人的火塘。
世界的中心,一个巨大的圆。

十八

吉狄普夷③的一生,
都未离开过自己的村庄。
但他的每句话里,
却在讲述这个世界别的地方。

十九

鹰飞到了一个极限,
身体在最后一个瞬间毁灭。
它没有让我们看见,
一次无穷和虚无完整的过程。

16

I climb onto god's back
Wanting to tell him a riddle,
But I hover asleep like a salmon
In water lit by the glow of dawn.

17

The hearth of the Nuosu—
At the world's center, a gigantic ring.

18

In Jidi Puyi's lifetime[④]
He never left his home district,
But everything he said
Gave an account of the world's ways.

19

The eagle flew to the furthest limit,
To its final moment of physical destruction;
It did not allow anyone to see
That culmination of infinity and emptiness.

二十

在天地之间，
我是一个圆点，当时间陷落，
我看见天空上
浮现出空无的胎记。

二十一

是谁占有了他的口腔，
让他的舌头唱得发麻。
这个歌者已经传了五十七代，
不知下一次会选择哪一个躯壳？

二十二

谁让群山在那里齐唱，
难道是英雄支呷阿鲁[④]？
不朽者横陈大地之上，
让我们把返程的缰绳攥紧。

二十三

银匠尔古[⑤]敲打着银子，
一只只蝴蝶在别的体内苏醒。
虽然他早已辞世不在人间，
但他的敲击还在叮当作响。

20

Between sky and earth
I am a round point, and when time capsizes
I see the birthmark of emptiness
Emerging across the heavens.

21

For whoever gains possession of his windpipe,
Let songs come forth until his tongue turns numb.
As singer he has come down through 57 generations;
Who knows which fleshly envelope will be chosen next?

22

Who makes the ranged mountains sing in unison?
Could it be the hero Zhyge Alu?[5]
That enduring one still lies across this land,
Tightening our grip on reins of the homeward journey.

23

As the silversmith Ergu[6] taps out shapes in silver
Butterflies tremble to life in someone else's body.
Though he has bid farewell to the land of the living,
His busy tip-tapping is still heard among us.

二十四

那只名字叫沙洛⑥的狗,
早已死亡,现在
只是一个影子。
它被时间的锯齿,
割出了声音和血。

二十五

我们曾把人分成若干的等级。
这是历史的错误。但你能不能
把本不属于我的两件东西,
现在就拿走。

二十六

我想念苦荞的时候,
嘴里却有毒品的滋味。
我拒绝毒品的时候,
眼前却有苦荞的幻影。

二十七

掘金者在那高原的深处,
挖出了一个巨大的矿坑。
这是罪证。但伤口缄默无语。

24

That long- dead dog named Shalo[7]
Is just a shadow now;
A rasp of bloody sawteeth
Separates it from us in time.

25

It was our historical mistake to divide people
Into this or that caste. Now I have two things
That did not originally belong to me.
Can you take them from me right away?

26

When the taste of illegal drugs is in my mouth
I miss the taste of bitter buckwheat.
When I refuse to take illegal drugs
Visions of ripe buckwheat appear before me.

27

There were gold diggers deep in the highlands;
They excavated a deep pit there.
This was proof of crime, but wounds keep silent.

二十八

他们骑马巡视自己的领地，
就是在马背上手端一杯酒
也不会洒落下半滴。
而我们已经没有这种本事。

二十九

没有人敢耻笑我的祖辈。
因为从生到死，
他们的头颅和目光都在群山之上。

三十

拥有谚语和格言，
就是吞下了太阳和火焰。
德古⑦坐在火塘的上方，
他的语言让世界进入了透明。

三十一

不是每一本遗忘在黑暗中的书，
都有一个词被光亮惊醒。
死亡的胜利，又擦肩而过。

28

They rodeon horses to inspect their territory;
On horseback they held their cups level
Not spilling a drop of wine;
Now we have lost the knack of this.

29

No one dared to laugh at my forefathers,
Because all through their lives
Their heads had mountaintops for a vantage point.

30

Having a fund of proverbs and maxims
Meant you could swallow sun and fire.
Elders sat on the hearth's upper side;[8]
Their words brought the world into transparency.

31

Not every book forgotten in darkness
Contains a word that was startled awake by light;
Death's victories pass by, rubbing shoulders with them.

三十二

吹拂的风在黑暗之上,
黑暗的浮板飘荡在风中,
只有光,唯一的存在,
能回到最初的时日。

三十三

寂静的群山,
只有天堂的反光,能让我们看见
雪的前世和今生。

三十四

只有光能引领我们,
跨越深渊,长出翅膀,
成为神的使者。
据说光只给每个人一次机会。

三十五

我没有抓住时间的缰绳,
但我却幸运地骑上了光的马背。
额头是太阳的箭镞,命令我:
杀死了死亡!

32

Caressing air blows overhead in darkness,
A dark raft drifts before the wind.
Only light, the be- all of existence
Can return to the time of origin.

33

Amid the stillness of ranged mountains
Only light reflected from heaven lets us see
The past and present lifetimes of snow.[9]

34

Only light can guide us
To cross over the abyss, to grow wings
And become god's messengers.
Some say the light gives each person only one chance.

35

I did not grab hold of time's reins,
But with luck I mounted a horse of light.
The blaze on its forehead is the sun's arrow- tip;
It commands me: "Go and slaughter death."

三十六

永恒的存在，除了依附于
黑暗，就只能选择光。
但我知道，只有光能从穹顶的高处，
打开一扇未来的窗户。

三十七

从群山之巅出发，
难道无限可以一分为二。
不是咒语所能阻止，
谁能分开那无缝的一。

三十八

星座并非独自滑动，
寂静的银河神秘异常。
风吹动着永恒的黑暗，
紧闭的侧门也被风打开。

三十九

巨石的上面：
星群的动与静，打开了手掌的纹路，
等待指令，返回最初的子宫。

36

Eternal being, aside from clinging to darkness
Can only choose the light.
At the height of heaven's vault, I know,
Only light can open the door to tomorrow.

37

To take mountain peaks as the point of departure:
Would this be dichotomizing infinity?
This is not something a mantra can hold back…
Who can divide up seamless oneness?

38

Constellations do not slide along on their own;
The silent Milky Way is the strangest mystery.
As wind stirs in eternal darkness...
It blows open side doors that were once sealed.

39

Above a megalith,
Star clusters deploy the creases of a palm- print;
They wait to be dispatched—back to the original womb.

四十

在大地上插上一根神枝，
遥远的星空就有一颗星熄灭。
那是谁的手？在插神枝。

四十一

母鸡一直啼鸣
还有野鸟停在了屋上。
明天的旅行是否还要启程？
我只听从公鸡的鸣叫。

四十二

不能在室内备鞍，
那是一种禁忌。
我的骏马跃入了云层，
蹄子踩在了羽毛上。

四十三

阿什拉则不是一个哑巴，
只是生性沉默。
是他独自在林中消遣，
创造了词语的乳房和钥匙。

40

A sacred branch is inserted in the good earth;
In sidereal space, right then, a star burns out.
Whose hand is the sacred branch inserted by?

41

A hen clucks constantly;
A grouse perches on the roof.
Should a journey commence tomorrow?
I only listen for the rooster's crowing.

42

Do not keep a saddle indoors:
That would go against our taboo.
My steed leaps into the clouds,
Its hooves treading upon feathers.

43

Ashylazzi was not a deaf- mute;
His temperament was innately silent.
He caused words to give milk
and created a key for them.

四十四

据说我们放羊的地方,
牛羊看见的景色还是那样。
但见不到你的身影,
从此这里只留下荒凉。

四十五

谁碰落了草茎上那颗露水,
它在地上砸出了一个巨大的深坑。

四十六

我愿意为那群山而去赴死,
数千年来并非只有我一人。

四十七

羊子被卖到远方,
魂魄在今夜还会回到栏圈。
我扔出去的那块石头,
再没有一点回声。

四十八

黄蜂在山岩上歌唱,

44

It is said that in our pasture grounds
Cows and sheep saw the same scenes as always,
But they never saw your looming shape;
Since then only waste ground remains here.

45

Who bumped that dewdrop loose from a blade of grass?
It slammed into the ground and made a huge pit.

46

For the sake of ranged mountains
I am willing to ride forth and meet death;
Over thousands of years, I haven't been the only one.

47

Sheep were sold to a faraway place;
Tonight their wraiths return to the corral.
The stone I throw into the darkness
No longer stirs an answering sound.

48

Hornets sing on a cliff- side,

不能辜负了金色的阳光。
明年同样美好的时辰,
只有雏鹰在这里筑巢。

四十九

那匹独角马日行千里,
但今天它却待在马厩里。
只有它的四蹄还在奔跑,
这是另一种游戏。

五十

我是世界的一个榫头,
没有我,宇宙的脊椎会发出
吱呀的声响。

五十一

金黄的四只老虎,
让地球在脚下转动。
我在一条大河的旁边成眠,
潜入了老虎的一根胡须。

五十二

因为你,时间让河流
获得了静止和不朽。
它的名字叫底坡夷莫⑧,

Not lettinggolden sunlight go to waste.
Next year at this halcyon hour,
Only eaglets will have their nest here.

49

Once it ran three hundred miles in a day,
Now that magical steed remains in the stable.
Galloping of hooves can only go on
By changing to another game.

50

I am a dowel of the world:
Without me the backbone of the cosmos
Would make a creaky, grating sound.

51

Four golden tigers
Spin the earth beneath their feet.
While dozing beside a big river
I sneak onto a tiger's whisker.

52

Because you are here, time casts a placid spell
On the river's enduring current.
It is named Ddipoyymo;[10]

没有波澜，高贵而深沉。

五十三

我们是雪族十二子，
六种植物和六种动物。
诸神见证过我们。但唯有人
杀死过我们其中的兄弟。

五十四

山中细细的竖笛，
彝人隐秘的脊柱。
吹响生命，也吹响死亡。

五十五

阿什拉则和吉狄马加，
有时候是同一个人。
他们的声音，来自于群山的合唱。

五十六

欢乐是死亡的另一种胜利，
没有仪式，就没法证明。

五十七

我是吉狄·略且·马加拉格，

Its noble, profound flow does not churn and froth.

53

I am a son of the Twelve Snow Tribes:[11]
Six of them are plant and six are animal...
The gods bear witness to us, but only we human beings
Have slaughtered our brother creatures.

54

In the mountains, a vertical flute as thin as a reed
Is the hidden backbone of the Nuosu;
It blows sounds of death; it blows sounds of life.

55

Ashylazzi and Jidi Majia
Are sometimes the same person.
Their voice comes from the chorus of ranged mountains.

56

Jubilation is death's victory in alternate form;
Without a ritual there is no proof.

57

I am Jidi Laeqie Majia- lage;[12]

切开了血管。
请你先向我开枪,然后我再。
但愿你能打中我的心脏。

五十八

这里有血亲复仇的传统,
当群山的影子覆盖。
为父辈们欠下的命债哭号,
我的诗只颂扬自由和爱情。

五十九

不要依赖手中的缰绳,
矮种马是你忠实的伙伴。
是的,凭借虚无的存在,
它最终也能抵达火的土地。

六十

款待客人是我们的美德,
锅庄里的柴火照亮里屋顶。
快传递今天皮碗里的美酒,
明天的火焰留下的仍然是灰烬。

六十一

沙马乌芝^⑨是一个最好的
琴手,她的一生就是为了弹奏。

My veins have been opened;
Go ahead and shoot, then I will take my turn.
May your bullet find its mark in my heart.

58

We have a tradition of blood vendettas here
Even as the shadows of mountains cover us.
Wail as you may of blood debts from your father's era,
My poems only uphold freedom and love.

59

Don't depend too much on reins you hold:
That pony is your loyal companion.
Yes, put your trust in a being that is nothing;
In the end it will arrive at the land of fire.

60

Hospitality is one of our virtues;
Our hearth fire lights the roof- beams.
Now it's time to pass the leather wine bowl;
Only ashes will remain of tonight's flames.

61

Shama Vyzyr[13] was best at playing moon guitar;
She lived to pluck the strings.

据说她死去的那天,
琴弦独自断在风中。

六十二

院子里的那只小猫,
不知道生命的荒诞。
它在玩弄一只老鼠,
让现实具有了意义。

六十三

祭司在人鬼之间,
搭起了白色的梯子。
举着更高的烟火,
传递着隔界的消息。

六十四

我梦见妈妈正用马勺,
从金黄的河流里舀出蜂蜜。
灿烂的阳光和风,
吹乱了妈妈的头发。

六十五

饮过鹰爪杯的嘴唇,
已经无法算清。
我们是世界的匆匆过客,

It is said that on the day she died,
A string of her yuo qi broke in the wind, all by itself.

62

That kitty in the courtyard
Knows nothing of life's absurdity.
It is toying with a mouse,
To give the afternoon a little meaning.

63

The priest erects a white ladder
Between human beings and ghosts.
He raises a smoke column high
To send tidings into the next world.

64

I dreamed my mother was using a ladle,
Scooping honey from a golden river.
There was splendor in the sunlight,
And wind was tousling her hair.

65

They are past counting, those lips
That drank from an eagle- talon goblet.
We are passers- by in this world;

今天它又有了新的主人。

六十六

我试图用手中的网，
去网住沉重的时间。
但最终被我网住的
却是真实的虚无。

六十七

你的意识不进入这片语言的疆域，
你的快马就不可能抵达词的中心。

六十八

我要去没有城墙的城市。
并非我们双腿和心灵缺少自由。

六十九

不是你发现了我。
我一直在这里。

七十

传说是狗的尾巴捎来了一粒谷种，
否则不会有山下那成片的梯田。

New owners are taking over now.

66

I cast the net in my hands
Hoping to gather in a weighty interval,
But what I ended up catching
Was genuine nothingness.

67

Unless your awareness crosses the rangeland of language,
Your fast horse will never reach the heart of a word.

68

I want to go to a city without city walls;
By no means do my legs and spirit lack freedom.

69

It was not you who discovered me;
I have been here all the while.

70

Legend says a kernel of grain hitched a ride on a dog's tail,
Otherwise these foothills wouldn't have terraced fields.

据说这次你带来的是偶然，
而不是争论不休的巧合。

七十一

我没有被钉在想象的黑板上，
不是我侥幸逃脱。
而是阿什拉则问我的时候，
我能如实地回答。

七十二

妇人背水木桶里游着小鱼，
屋后养鸡鸡重十二斤。
曾是炊烟不断的祖居地，
但如今它只存活于幽暗的词语。

七十三

我虽喜欢黑红黄三种颜色，
很多时候，白色也是我的最爱。
但还是黑色，
更接近我的灵魂。

七十四

一条金色的河流，穿过了未来，
平静，从容，舒缓，没有声音。
它覆盖梦的时候，也覆盖了泪水。

Some say this time you've brought along a random chance,
Not a coincidence that needs all kinds of explaining.

71

I was never fastened to an imaginary blackboard,
So I won't claim that lucklet me break free.
Anyway, when Ashylazzi questioned me,
I answered according to the way things are.

72

Little fish darted in waterpails carried by women;
Chickens in the backyard weighed twelve pounds;
In that ancestral place, kitchen fires never ceased;
All are only kept alive now in dim recesses of words.

73

Though I like the colors black, red and yellow,
There are times when I am fondest of white,
But the color black, after all,
Is closest to my soul.

74

A golden river flows through the future,
Tranquil and soundless, serene and unhurried.
It covers up dreams and at the same time covers up tears.

七十五

我要回去,但我回不去
正因为回不去,才要回去。

七十六

我要到撒拉底坡⑩去,
在那里耍七天七夜。
在这七天七夜,我爱所有的人,
但只有一人是我的唯一。

七十七

彝谚说,粮食中的苦荞最大,
昨天我还吃过苦荞。
但我的妈妈已经衰老,
还有谁见过她少女时的模样?

七十八

我不会在这光明和黑暗的时代,
停止对太阳的歌唱,
因为我的诗都受孕于光。

七十九

时间在刀尖上舞蹈,

75

I want to go back, but I cannot;
Just because I cannot go back, I want to go.

76

I want to go to Sala Ndipo[14]
In that place I will while away seven days and nights.
All through those seven days and nights, I will love everyone,
Keeping in mind who is my one and only.

77

The Yi proverb says, "Among foodstuffs bitter buckwheat is unrivalled."
Only yesterday I ate bitter buckwheat,
But my mother is frail with age.
Who among the living has seen her girlish appearance?

78

In this era of darkness and brightness
I will not stop singing of the sun,
Because my poetry was impregnated by light.

79

Time does its dance on the tip of a knife;

只有光能刺向未来。

八十

格言在酒樽中复活,
每一句都有火焰的滋味。

八十一

我钻进世界的缝隙,
只有光能让我看见死去的事物。

八十二

失去了属于我的马鞍,
我只能用灵魂的翅膀飞翔。

八十三

我的母语在黑暗里哭泣,
它的翅膀穿越了黎明的针孔。

八十四

我在火焰和冰雪之间徘徊,
这个瞬间无异于已经死亡。

Only light pierces into the future.

80

Proverbs come to life in a pitcher of wine;
Every sentence has the flavor of flames.

81

I burrow into the world's cracks;
Only light lets me see what has died.

82

Having lost the saddle that belonged to me,
I can only fly on wings of spirit.

83

My mother tongue sobs in the darkness;
Its wings had to pass through the needle's eye of dawn.

84

I waver between flames and icy snow;
This moment is no different than being dead.

八十五

光明和黑暗统治世界,
时光的交替不可更改。
只有死亡的长风传来密令,
它们是一对孪生的姐妹。

八十六

那是消失的英雄时代,
诸神和勇士都在巡视群山。
沉静的天空寂寥深远,
只有尊严战胜了死亡和时间。

八十七

我不会在别处向这个世界诀别,
只能在群山的怀抱,时间在黎明。
当火焰覆盖我的身体,
我会让一只鸟告诉你们。

八十八

我不会给这个世界留下咒语,
因为人类间的杀戮还没有停止。
我只能把头俯向尘土,
向你耳语:忘记仇恨。

85

Brightness and darkness rule the world;
Their alternations in time cannot be changed.
Death's steady wind brings a secret message:
They are a pair of twin sisters.

86

In that bygone era of heroes,
Gods and warriors patrolled the mountains.
The silent sky was a remote void;
Only dignity won out over death and time.

87

I will not take leave of this world anywhere else—
Only in the embrace of mountains, at the hour of dawn.
As flames engulf my body
I will send a bird to tell you...

88

I will leave no incantations in this world,
Because slaughter is still going on.
I can only lower my head toward the dust
And whisper to you: "Forget hatred."

八十九

当整个人类绝望的时候，
我们不能绝望。
因为我们是人类。

九十

我的声音背后还有声音。
那是成千上万的人的声音。
是他们合成了一个人的声音。
我的声音。

九十一

直到有一天这个世界
认同了我的价值，
黑暗才会穿过伤口，
让自己也成为光明的一个部分。

九十二

真理坐在不远的地方
望着我们。阿格索祖⑪也在那里。
当我们接近它的时候，
谬误也坐在了旁边。

89

Even when humankind as a whole despairs,
We cannot despair,
Because we are humankind.

90

Behind my voice there are other human sounds—
Sounds made by hundreds and thousands of people;
All their voices are compounded into one,
And that is my voice.

91

If the day ever comes when this world
Finally recognizes my value,
Darkness will pass out of my wounds,
And at last I can be part of the light.

92

Truth sits in a place not far away
Watching us. Agishyzu is there also,[15]
But when we get anywhere close,
Fallacy is also sitting beside them.

九十三

我从某一个时日醒来，
看见九黄星值守着天宇。
不是八卦都能预言人的吉凶，
诗歌只赞颂日月永恒的运行。

九十四

我不知道布鲁洛则山⑫在哪里？
如同不知道天空中的风变幻的方向。
在漆黑的房里，透过火塘的微光，
我似乎第一次看到了生命真实的存在。

九十五

从一开始就不是为自己而活着，
所以我敢将一把虚拟的匕首，
事先插入了心中。

九十六

我的心灵布满了伤痕，
却用微笑面对这个世界。
如果真的能穿过时间的缝隙，
或许还能找到幸运的钥匙。

93

I wake from the day and the hour to see
The Nine Yellow Stars presiding in heaven.[16]
Not all divination is done to reveal people's fortunes;
Poetry only praises eternal motions of sun and moon.

94

I don't know where Bbylozzibbo Mountain is,[17]
Or which quarter the next wind will blow from.
No matter how dark the room, by light of embers I discern,
Sooner than most, how existence is for my fellow beings.

95

From the start I haven't lived for myself,
So I dare to grasp a virtual dagger ahead of time
And plunge it into my heart.

96

My heart is covered with scars
Yet I face this world with a smile.
If I could really pass through a crack in time,
Perhaps I could find the key to happiness.

九十七

在那片树林里有一只鸽子,
它一直想飞过那紫色的山尖。
唯一担心的是鹞鹰的突然出现,
生与死在空中留下了一个偌大的空白。

九十八

降生时妈妈曾用净水为我洗浴,
诀别人世还有谁能为我洗去污垢。
这个美好而肮脏的世界,
像一滴水转瞬即逝。

九十九

虎豹走过山林,花纹
在身后熠熠生辉。
我拒绝了一个词的宴请,
但却接受了一万句克哲⑬的约会。

一〇〇

拥着马鞍而眠,
词语的马蹄铁发出清脆的响声。
但屋外的原野却一片空寂。

97

In the grove there is a dove
With hopes of flying to a distant, bluish peak.
Its only worry is that a hawk would suddenly appear:
Death would leave blankness in air where life once was.

98

At my birth, Mother bathed me with pure water;
When I leave this world, someone will cleanse me of grime.
This beautiful and dirty world
Is like a water drop, passing in a moment.

99

A big cat stalks the mountain forest;
Leaving the brilliance of its pattern behind.
I refused an invitation to the banquet of a single word,
But made a date for a flyting of 10, 000 sentences.[18]

100

Asleep with my arms around a saddle…
Words are horseshoes clopping in my ears,
But outside of the house lies a silent wasteland.

一〇一

头上的穹顶三百六十度,
吹动着永恒的清气和浊气。
生的门和死的门,都由它们掌管。
别人只能旁观。

一〇二

从瓦板房的缝隙,
能看见灿烂浩瀚的星空。
不知星群的上面是屋顶还是晨曦。
这是一个难题,也是另一个或许。

一〇三

世界上的万物有生有灭,
始终打开的是生和死的门户。
我与别人一样,死后留下三魂[14],
但我有一魂会世代吟唱诗歌。

101

The 360 degrees of heaven forever stir
With gusts of pure and turbid energy,
Holding mastery over doors of life and death.
Anyone else is an onlooker.

102

From cracks in a plank-roofed house
Glimmers from the starry heavens show through.
Could there be another roof above the stars, or just daybreak?
This is an enigma, and it is another maybe.

103

Myriad things of the world take birth and die;
The gates of life and death are always open.
Like others, I will leave three souls after death,[19]
But one of them will chant poetry through the ages.

①毕摩，彝族中的祭司和文字传承者。

②三星堆，中国西部一著名的文化遗址。

③吉狄普夷，彝族部族中一个人的名字。

④支呷阿鲁，彝族传说中的创世英雄。

⑤尔古，彝族历史上一位银匠的名字。

⑥沙洛，彝族历史上一只狗的名字。

⑦德古，彝族中智者和德高望重的人。

⑧底坡夷莫，彝族群山腹地一条著名的河流，常被用来形容女性。

⑨沙马乌芝，彝族民间一位著名的月琴手。

⑩撒拉底坡，彝族火把节一处著名的聚会地。

⑪阿格索祖，彝族历史上著名的祭司和智者。

⑫布鲁洛则山，彝区一座著名的山脉，据说在云南境内。

⑬克哲，彝族一种古老的诗歌对答形式。

⑭三魂，彝人认为人死后有三魂，一魂留火葬处，一魂被供奉，一魂被送到祖先的最后归宿地。

①*Jidi Majia completed this suite of poems shortly after the Torch Festival in 2016. The Torch Festival is celebrated throughout Liangshan Yi Minority Prefecture around the time of the summer solstice.* —Tr.

②*Abimo is a priest who performs rituals and chants sacred texts. In traditional Yi society, bimos are males, and the right to become a bimo is hereditary, passing from father to son.*

③*Sanxing Mound is an archaeological site found near Guanghan City, Sichuan. Bronze masks and vessels from the mound are thought to date back 3000–5000 years.*

④*Jidi Puyi was a wise elder and townsman of the poet's father.* —Tr.

⑤*Zhyge Alu was a mythic hero of the Yi people whose deeds are recounted in an eponymous epic and in the Hnewo Teyy (Book of Origins).*

⑥*Ergu was the name of a master silversmith in Yi tradition.*

⑦*"Shalo" is the name of a dog that the poet remembers from childhood.* —Tr.

⑧*TheNuosu word ndeggu (in Chinese degu 德古) refers to persons of broad experience who are called in to give advice and mediate disputes.* —Tr.

⑨*TheNuosu word for "snow" is etymologically related to apuwasa—the spirit/daimon epitomizing a family's or individual's highest aspirations and virtues.* —Tr.

⑩*Ddipoyymo is a famous river in the heartland of Greater Liangshan. It is often referred to in descriptions of female beauty.*

⑪*According to Book of Origins, earthly life originated in a region of much snow, and each species fell into one of Twelve Tribes.* —Tr.

⑫*Jidi Lueqie Majia-Lage is the poet's full name. "Jidi" is his family name; "Lueqie" is his patronymic; "Majia" is his personal name; "Lage" is his baby name (used only by close relatives).* —Tr.

⑬*Shama Vyzyr was a famous player of the moon guitar (Chinese, yueqin; Nuosu, yuoqi).*

⑭*Sala Ndipo is a famous gathering place where Yi people celebrate the Torch Festival.*

⑮*Agishyzu was traditionally famous as a priest and wise man among*

233

the Yi.

⑯*The Nine Yellow Stars are an asterism in which each of the stars exerts influence in sequence according to a numerological system which integrates the Chinese luoshu (a nine-number square used in divination) with the ten month solar calendar of the Yi Minority. This asterism is mentioned in an astrological text titled Tuludouji*《土鲁窦吉》[*Generation of the Cosmos*]*, translated from the Yi language into Chinese by Wang Ziguo* 王子国 (*Guizhou Minorities Press* 1998). *The "Preface" by Guizhou Province Yi Studies Assn. President Lu Wenbin* 录文斌 *discusses Nine Yellow Stars in relation to divinatory trigrams and calendrical periods.* —Tr.

⑰*Bbylozzibbo is a mountain range often mentioned among the Yi as a geographical feature. It is said to be located in Yunnan Province.*

⑱ "*Flyting*" *refers to a verbal sparring match in which participants vie to outdo each other in wit, imagination, and grasp of proverbial expressions. In Yi society these matches are held on celebratory or convivial occasions. The Nuosu term which corresponds to "flyting" is kne-re or knep-rep.* —Tr.

⑲*The Yi people believe that after death a person has three souls. The first returns to be among one's ancestors; the second receives offerings (which are placed before a memorial plaque); the third remains at the cremation ground. The Nuosu names of the three souls are hlayi, hlajju, and hlage (literally defined as "wise soul," "half-wise soul," and "unwise soul").* —Tr.

下篇

"柔刚诗歌奖"颁奖会上的致答辞

尊敬的柔刚先生、尊敬的各位评委、朋友们：

感谢第二十届"柔刚诗歌奖"评委会把这个尊贵的奖项颁发给我，为此我充满了由衷的感激之情。我想大家也许能理解我这种感激的真正缘由，那就是这个诗歌奖项的设立者，包括它的评委会，无一例外都来自于民间，他们都是真正意义上的公共知识分子。我不知道今天在中国还有哪一项诗歌奖已经连续评选了二十届，并且一直还保持着它最初创立时所坚守的公正立场，而从不被诗歌之外的一切因素干扰和影响，这不能不说是个奇迹。我们可以想象，这个来自民间的诗歌奖能如此顽强地坚守到今天，其中必定会有许多鲜为人知的动人故事，但对于那些真正献身于诗歌的人们，这些他们所经历过的一切，似乎早已被深深埋藏在了记忆的深处，而这种经历本身，毫无疑问已经赋予了他们的人生一种更为特殊的意义。作为同行，在这里我们没有理由不对他们肃然起敬。

我要对他们表达诗歌的敬意，但我需要声明的是，我的这种敬意，完全来自于我们共同的对于诗歌纯粹的忠诚，而并不仅仅因为我是一个获奖者，如果真的是那样的话，那将是彻头彻尾的对人类诗歌精神的亵渎和不敬。我向他们表达敬意，那是因为在这个诗歌被极度边缘化的时代，对诗歌的热爱和坚持，仍然是需要勇气和奉献的。

当然，对于那些诗神的真正信徒来说，这并非就是一个事实，因为真理早已经告诉过我们，精神上伟大的孤独者和引领者，从来就是这个

Reply to the 20 Rougang Poetry Award Ceremony

Respected Mr. Rougang, respected jury, friends:

Gratitude overwhelms me when the notification came that the Rougang Award Jury decided to make me the recipient of the 20th Rougang Award. For a very solid reason in that the initiators of distinction, i. e. Mr Rougang, including its jury, has nothing to do with the establishment. They are truly of the civic society, the intellectuals in Zola's tradition, that is, with a heart for the downtrodden as well as an eye for knowledge genuinely worthy in the crowd. Who can tell me, in present day China, other than Rougang Award, there is any civic honor of poetry continuously running into its 20th occasions without compromising its original principles of non- discrimination and justice, undeterred by any non- poetic circumstances or factors from either political or commercial interests, a record nothing short of a miracle. One easily senses there should be heroes unsung and stories barely told in heeding such indomitable code of heroism. Everything unspeakable they have weathered being now conveniently hid deep in the recesses of their staunch psyche, such happenings are bound to imbue their lives with a special significance. As peers, I must rise, with cap in hand, to look them in the eyes with reverence and amazement.

I must show them due respects, in the like- minded companionship, but this I must add, as my respects emanate totally from a common devotion to the art of poetry, by no means a gesture of the vested interests, i. e. being glorified by this award. And if this being true, I stand justified of profanity and disloyalty to the human spirit in the highest degree. To openly acknowledge my gratitude is tantamount to claiming my firm bond with true lovers of Pushkin and Shakespeare as well as my unshakable faith in poetry in a wholesale prosaic age given to unscrupulous pursuit of trite objects of life, such as luxury and outward ostentation, lampooned one century ago by giants like Einstein as the ethical basis of pigsty.

Yet, this plague spot of civilization ought to be neutralized and checked with all possible speed and means, although I am deeply aware of the fact for

世界的极少数，或许正是因为有这样一群人的精神守望，我们才从未怀疑过诗歌是人类存在下去的最有说服力的理由。因为诗歌包含了人性中最美最善的全部因素，它本身就是想象的化身，它是语言所能表达的最为精微的秘密通道。

诗歌从诞生之日起，它就和我们的灵魂以及生命本体中，最不可捉摸的那一部分厮守在一起，从某种意义上说，诗歌是我们通过闪着泪光的心灵，在永远不可知晓的神秘力量的感召下，被一次次唤醒的隐藏在浩瀚宇宙和人类精神空间里的折射和倒影。我们彝族人中最伟大的精神和文化传承者毕摩，就是用这种最古老的诗歌方式，完成了他们与宇宙万物以及神灵世界的沟通和对话。他们是诗人中的祭司，他们是人类诗歌无可争辩的先行者。

当然，我还想要告诉大家的是，诗歌语言所构建的世界，一直被认为是诗人的另一个更为隐秘的领域，它是所有伟大诗人必须经历的，有时甚至是无法预知的文字探险，从这个角度上来看，这个世界上所有的文字掌握者，他们在文字的最为精妙、最为复杂、最为不可思议的创造方面，都将永远无法与天才的诗人们比肩。诗人毫无争议地是语言王国中当之无愧的国王。有人曾经说过这样的话，诗歌的语言就是稀有的金属和珍奇的宝石，在文字和声音中最完美的呈现。

朋友们，在此时我还想与大家分享的是，最近我有机会刚刚完成了一次诗歌与朝圣的远游。我有幸应邀到南美秘鲁参加二十世纪最伟大的诗人之一，塞萨尔·巴列霍诞辰一百二十周年的纪念活动，最令我感动的是，当我们深入到安第斯山区的腹部，来到这位有着印第安血统的诗人的故乡时，我惊奇地发现就是在这样一个极为偏僻、遥远和封闭的世界里，诗歌的力量和影响也从未消失。塞萨尔·巴列霍，这位写出了迄今为止人类有关心灵苦难最为深刻的诗歌的诗人，用他忧伤的诗句，再一次为我们印证了古罗马诗人贺拉斯的名言，诗歌的生命要比青铜的寿

human civilization to achieve any level of decency, there must be some great loners and leaders, poets among them, categorically in the minority, who stand on vigil for the sanity of human cultures and whose presence speaks volumes about the fittest of the survival of human race across the globe simply because poetry contains the unique essence of man as man, i. e. the true and the good, the simulation of human dignity and imagination, the most sophisticated channels of verbal beauty and sophistry.

Ever at the dawn of humanity, poetry was with us, an integral part of our inner being. In a sense, poetry is, with religion, the most beautiful and mysterious experience we possess, activated time and again by a force whose power and origin is totally inaccessible to our minds, a refraction or a reflection of the Almighty cosmic Gesit. We in our Yi communities still retain our age- old awe for our shamans figures, that is, Bimos who always poetize and communion with all the sentient beings on earth and the deities. You call them priests, but to us Yi, they are also poets, the undisputed forerunners of human songs and epics.

Of course, I must impart this occultist knowledge to my fellow poets that Utopia made of poetic diction is an invisible realm from and across whose bourn very few poets have the luck to tour and sightsee around. It is frankly an adventure or venture into the unknown, the supremely aesthetic. I console myself, even of all the most remarkable and dainty human creations, all the craftsmen specialized and good at words, poets emerge supreme and divine. Poets are beyond argument the kings of all letters of men and women. Somebody asserts, with full assurance, poetry is diamond among the richest stones and the most precious metals of human spirituality, the perfect synchronization of sound and word in the best order.

Friends, I shall open my heart to you with a pilgrimage of poetry I have conducted not long ago. As luck would have it, I was invited to Mexico to attend the celebrations of the 120th anniversary of the birth of César Vallejo, one of the greatest bards Latin America has ever seen. What impressed me most, when taken to César Vallejo's hometown in the heartland of the Andes, so unbelievably distant, isolated and backwater, poetry still has a tenacious hold upon local inhabitants. Cesar Vallejo, from whose mouth such movingly plaintive songs issue, of the human sorrows and joys in superlatives, has been one

命更为久长。

在诗人的故乡圣地亚哥·德·丘科这个古老的区域,当我们目睹了他的一个又一个土著族人背诵他的诗篇时,眼睛里面流露出的尊严和自信,无疑深深地震撼了我们。尽管作为一位彻底颠覆了一般诗歌语言的大师,读者要真正进入他所设置的语言迷宫并非易事,但他的诗歌所透示出来的人道主义情怀、对弱者和被剥削者的同情,以及他对生命、死亡的永不停歇的追问,都会触动这个世界上,任何一个还保留着良知和道德认同的人的心弦。

塞萨尔·巴列霍曾写下过这样的诗句,"白色的石头上,压着一块黑色的石头",我知道这是他在用诗歌,对永恒的死亡在哲学层面上的最后祭奠和定格。塞萨尔·巴列霍已经离开我们七十四年了,但是我们从没有过这样的感觉:他的生命已经真的死亡。作为一个精神上和肉体上的双重流放者,他至死都没有再回到自己的故乡,但让我们略感欣慰的是,时间做出了最为公正的判决,他不朽的诗歌正延续着他短暂的足以让人悲泣的肉体生命。塞萨尔·巴列霍是安第斯山里的一块巨石,但在今天他也是一位享誉世界的杰出公民。他的一生和光辉的诗篇给了我们一个启示,那就是真正伟大的诗歌和诗人,是任何邪恶势力都永远无法战胜的。因为诗人和诗歌永远只面临一种考验,那就是无情的时间和一代又一代的读者。再次感谢各位评委的慷慨之举,我无以回报,但请相信我,在诗神面前,我将永远是一位谦卑忠实的仆人。

谢谢大家!

of the most recent showcases in evidence to the forcible truthfulness of Horace's adage, the Roman laureate poet: poetry endures longer than bronze.

In Santiago de Chuco, a remote village in the Peruvian Andes. I saw with my own eyes, one by one, his tribesmen, recited his poems, there was a note of dignity in their voices, an expression of solemn ecstasy on their faces. It was a scene that shocked and captivated. Considered one of the great poetic innovators of the 20th century in any language, very few readers find it an easy task to extricate themselves from his labyrinth. yet, his profound sympathy for the incarcerated and the insulted, his born humanitarianism and his relentless probing into the most stubborn issues of life and death have left the whole world awed and inspired, poets and ordinary readers who still are vulnerable to questioning of conscience mingled with good sense and good feeling. César Vallejo once wrote: " A black stone laid upon a white stone." He was penning his own epigraph in poetic diction, nay, he was philosophizing ultimately on the meaning of death.

74 years have elapsed since César Vallejo, the most radically avant- garde poet in the 20th century, left us. Yet strangely, I never feel like he is gone. To me, he lives among us every minute of it. An exile physically and spiritually, perennially in dire poverty In Europe, he never returned to the fold of his home country. Yet his memory has been now vindicated that his fame has circled the earth, much to the consolation of all those who love his poems, as a gigantic rock in the Peruvian Andes, as a distinguished citizen of the world. His poetic legacy is a testament to his monumental greatness that great poets and lasting poetry must prevail upon al those dark and evil forces. Ultimately his story affords us the ultimate enlightenment that weak and facile poetry will not survive its weakling maker. Time will test which is which. With this at the tip of my tongue, I must stand guard on any from of self pity and self complacency and I must keep forging ahead with the greatest measure of humility and audacity in carrying on with my artistic endeavor.

Thank you all for your attention.

在为费尔南多·伦东·梅里诺颁发青海湖国际诗歌节国际诗歌交流贡献奖会上的致辞

各位女士、各位先生、诗人朋友们：

今天在这里，我非常荣幸地为费尔南多·伦东·梅里诺颁发青海湖国际诗歌节国际诗歌交流贡献奖，我以为这既是对他为当代国际诗歌交流贡献的一种肯定，同时也是为了更好地来进一步促进不同民族、不同国家、不同地域诗歌的交流。

关于费尔南多·伦东·梅里诺，不光是我们在座的许多朋友熟悉他，其实，早在二十年前，他就已经成为国际诗坛国际诗歌交流领域里一位十分活跃的组织者。前不久，他的一本诗集在中国出版，我在序言中曾这样写道：

费尔南多·伦东·梅里诺在当今世界诗坛，无疑是一个带有标识性和符号性的人物，坦率地说，说他是一个带有标识性和符号性的人物，并不是讲他的诗歌作品在当今世界诗坛所占有的特殊位置，而是，他作为一个行动的诗人，在全球化背景下的世界诗歌运动中，所体现出来的无与伦比的显赫作用，以及他对当今进行的跨国界诗歌交流所做出的巨大贡献。

据我所知，他无疑是这样一个始终把行动看得更为重要，同时一直在把自己全部的力量和智慧，奉献给人类诗歌建设的人。毫无疑问，他是这个世界上我所了解和认识的，为推动当代诗歌发展和繁荣，众多的

Address to Fernando Rendon by Jidi Majia at the Ceremony of Presenting an Award in Honor of Fernando Rendon's Outstanding Contribution to Promote World Poetry Movement

Ladies and Gentlemen, Fellow Poets:

I am privileged today to present an award to Mr Fernando Rendon in recognition of his excellent leadership in promoting poetic expansion across our planet as a powerful tool for change, a token of our gratitude not only for him as such a charismatic leader in initiating two of the greatest contemporary cultural movements, i. e. International Poetry Festival of Medelin and WPM (World Poetry Movement), but also as a call for action to all our fellow poets, inspired by his example and wishing to emulate Fernando Rendon in furthering the grand cause of which the great Columbian has been such a rallying-point and a standard.

Regarding the Columbian whom we honor on this special occasion, I trust many of our friends in the audience know him quite intimately. In fact, back in the 1900s, F. R emerged to become a household name as promoter and central figure in organizing poetic events and boosting communications among world poets. Very recently, the first book of his verse has been published in China which I have prefaced thus:

The unmistakable towering personality of contemporary world poetry, the figure of Fernando Rendon has however, an even greater importance than lyrical talent warrants, that is, in the capacity of a poet in action, destiny has hoisted on his shoulders of leadership of world poetic movements in the present age of globalization, a function, as we all see so vividly, he has performed and officiated so admirably that earns him worldwide admiration and reverence.

To the best of my knowledge, Fernando Rendon's emergence has come at a difficult time of Columbian history when his home country has been bled by an almost half-century-long fratricidal wars. To the woes and burning issues of his country and the world, he has brought the resources of his powerful intellect. Poetry to him has naturally become a weapon in bringing an end to internal conflicts and social injustice, in the firm belief in a fair Colombian reconciliation, but also world peace made possible through protracted poetic actions in the ardent construction of a globe for poetry and for life. We feel compelled to honor him because he has contributed, like no one else, through

诗歌活动组织者中最为杰出的几个人物之一。

费尔南多·伦东·梅里诺就像一团火,他无论走到哪里,都在为诗歌而奔走呼号,因为他的努力,在哥伦比亚麦德林启动的"国际诗歌运动",才成为一个全球范围内的旨在为了促进和平、社会公正、人权和自然保护的跨文化行动,可以说,自诗歌诞生以来,还从未有过这样广泛的世界性的诗歌对话和交流,这一行动让诗歌在改变人类生命、重构更人道的人类价值体系,发挥了不可估量的作用。

面对今天这样一个被资本和技术操控的时代,把诗歌作为武器,并试图通过诗歌的传播和启蒙,来改变人类的生存方式,并为所有的生命找到通向明天的光明路径,在有些人看来,这完全是痴人妄想,但费尔南多·伦东·梅里诺却从未放弃这一追求和梦想,正因为在他身上所具有的这种永远不向任何邪恶势力妥协的高尚品质,他才取得了在常人看来,完全不可能取得的成功,也正是因为这一巨大的成功,他才成为了我们的从事诗歌运动的榜样。

鉴于费尔南多·伦东·梅里诺在国际诗歌交流中做出的贡献,特别是他始终将诗歌作为人类建设未来美好生活的武器,并从未放弃过对于这一理想的执着追求,青海湖国际诗歌节组委会,特别决定为他颁发青海湖国际诗歌节国际诗歌交流贡献奖。

inciting and organizing poetic activities in various forms, to a flourishing world poetry movement as we all are an active part of.

Afire with passion for spreading poetic joy, Fernando Rendon is a man born with a mission, which is poetry, with a divine message to carry across frontiers between nations, races and religions, which is poetry for peace and justice. In the wake of phenomenal success of the exemplary International Poetry Festival of Medelin, he has added luster and glory to the Muses by starting WPM in a more vigorous and multitudinous celebration of life and earth involving a truly global participation of poets worldwide enhancing the rise of "a new planetary awareness that shall promote urgent changes in the attitude of contemporary society" in the face of all the world crises to promote peace, social justice and ecological conservation. We might safely assume, no other lay person under the sun has achieved as much as our brilliant Fernando Rendon, the superb strategist of cultural movements, since the birth of poetry, in the way and momentum of spreading poetic joy and boosting communications among peer poets on such a massive scale. Increasingly WPM has been seen as a cataclysm in rebuilding human value systems and reorienting our lives towards a more humanistic tomorrow.

We are living in a world of manufactured needs, mass consumption and mass infotainment, driven by the aggregate preferences of capital lords and money chasers. To all this glitter of crass capitalism, Fernando Rendon turns his back by striking his bold blow and his method is nothing short of Herculean bravery as he trusts poets can work wonders and lead people onto a royal road of liberation and freedom. No wonder to some, Fernando Rendon is a modern Don Quixote, the idealistic dreamer who "assumes the power of poetry for change and urgent transformations" unabashedly, and Fernando Rendon's attempt at awakening people from their materialistic fetish through poetic readings resemble the exaggerated deeds of the 16th century's chivalric hero. But with what fortitude, strategic planning, and tact our modern Don Quixote has rallied allies and defied evil forces to emerge phenomenally successful to become a model we follow, an example we emulate.

Dear Fernando Rendon, on behalf of the Organizing Committee of Qinghai Lake International Poetry, I ask you to receive this Outstanding Contribution Award in honor of your decades of persistent and heroic striving for a better world through the medium of poetry.

青海湖国际诗歌节宣言

青海是人类诗和歌的最早摇篮之一，在长江、黄河和澜沧江的发源地，在苍茫的雪域高原，诗的圣灵之光，召唤我们来自中国和世界各国的诗人，会聚于中国美丽的青海湖畔，在这里见证一个事实，那就是以诗人的良知和诗歌的神圣，庄严发布青海湖诗歌宣言。

首先，我们确信，自远古至今，人类最伟大的精神创造就是拥有了诗歌。诗歌诞生于古代先民中的智者同神灵的对话和与自我的交流，因而诗歌是人类走出混沌世界的火把。诗歌是人类话语领域最古老的艺术形式，因而也是最具有生命力和感染力的艺术。无论过去还是现在，诗歌都是不可或缺的。它是滋润生命的雨露和照耀人性的光芒，只有它能用纯粹的语言，把一切所及之物升华为美。诗歌站在人类精神世界的前沿并且永远与人类精神生活中一切永恒的主题紧密相连。

回顾刚刚过去的一百年，人类为自己创造了太多的光荣，也酿制了太多的屈辱；经受了沉重的痛苦和灾难，也激发了一次又一次的历史变革和思想奋进！工具理性的飞速发展，充分开发了人类潜在的智能，把科学技术和物质文明推向了前所未有的高峰，人类在开发生存环境和开发自我的过程中，获得了前所未有的自由，同时我们的精神世界也变得

Manifesto of Qinghai Lake International Poetry

One of the earliest cradles of human songs, the fountain head of three China's mega waterways, Qinghai boasts a topographical position in the world's highest plateau, standing in pristine magnificence and hemmed in with poetic halo, luring and beckoning poets, thither and hither, far and wide, to gather by the shores of the holy Lake Koknor, bearing witness to a major cultural event. Today, we—this small migratory compact community of 220 poets from 23 counties, are lining lakeside to solemnly proclaim a manifesto, firmly affirmative of our poetic conscience as well as sanctity of poetic art.

First and foremost, we are convinced, since time immemorial, the most beautiful thing that happened to us humans is we are possessed of and by poetry, And thanks to the first generation of troubadours and ballad singers, man came out of chaos, striking out from the Jurassic jungle of the survival of the fittest into the dawn of civilization. Poetry took its origin from our ancient sages', prophets' and poets' dialogue with the deities, in their communion with themselves. Invariably the oldest art form within the compass of varied human discourse, poetry has proved to be the most vital and influential. It is inconceivable that man could have survived all the odds thrown his way without an inner prop like Illiad, Gesar or Book of Songs. Poetry is the raindrop that nurtures life, the sunshine that soothes melancholy, the ultimate divine force that purifies and uplifts human nature. A few inspired lines of Homer Li Bo and Shakespeare refine things around us and turn a stark coarse environment into a fairy land. Ever standing vigil in the forefront of human activity, poetry has been closely interwoven with all the cultural themes that make our spiritual life possible.

Looking back, the past century has seen an overflowing of human glory as well as of disgrace of his own making. There is too much undeserved suffering. There is also an abundance of divine- inspired redemption. Challenge is turned into opportunity, and crisis, into new impetus. The fermentation of Instrumental Rationality has led to a flourishing science and technology by tapping the huge potential latent in the inner recesses of the human psyche. In his efforts to harness and exploit nature, man has achieved the fullest measure of freedom which hangs heavy in his daring- all hands. On the other hand, overdependence

浮躁和窒息，对机器与技术的过分依赖，正在使我们的生命丧失主体性和原创力。

既然诗歌是民族文化的精粹和人类智慧的结晶，诗就应该是人类良知的眼睛，为此我们只有共同携起手来，弘扬诗歌精神，才能营造出人类精神家园的幸福与和谐。世界各国的诗人，虽然有着不同的宗教信仰和文化背景，却有一颗同样圣洁的诗心。现在，我们站在离太阳最近的地方，向全世界的诗人们呼唤：

在当今全球语境下，我们将致力于恢复自然伦理的完整性，我们将致力于达成文化的沟通和理解，我们将致力于维护对生活的希望和信念，我们将致力于推进人类之间的关爱和尊重，我们将致力于创建语言的纯洁和崇高。我们将以诗的名义反对暴力和战争，扼制灾难和死亡缔造人类多样化的和谐共存，从而维护人的尊严。我们将致力于构建人与自然、人与社会、人与文化、人与人之间的诗意和谐。这无疑是诗的责任，同样也是诗的使命。

我们永远也不会停止对诗歌女神的呼唤，我们在这里，面对圣洁的青海湖承诺：我们将以诗的名义，把敬畏还给自然，把自由还给生命，把尊严还给文明，让诗歌重返人类生活。

upon machine and computer has taken its toll, spawning a spiritual debasement and a choking of personality en masse, as well as a drastic decline in creativity in its wake.

But there is still hope and hope there is again found in poetry, the essence of human intellect and the eye of human conscience. For poets, regardless of origin or religion, are all endowed by the Creator with a pure poetic heart, throbbing and burning with a zest for Truth, Good and Beauty. At this moment, from where in closest proximity to the Sun, we appeal to all our counterparts and all those wishing to be enlightened afresh to lend us an ear for the proclamation of our manifesto.

We proclaim solemnly we will commit ourselves to restoring the integrity of a natural ethics governing human contact with nature, bridging of communication and understanding between cultures, upholding of the torch of the ancient hope of and faith in life and pushing for a globe where mutual respect, caring and love prevail.

We proclaim in deadly earnest that we shall undertake to purify language and exemplify poetic art in the name of which we oppose war to peace, justice to evil and with the means we excel, we will endeavor to deter suffering and death

Last but not the least, we will go all out to bring harmony to fruition, one that is essentially poetic by all accounts, cosmic in scope, deserving of human dignity, in refashioning a healthy and loving relationship involving all the sentient beings on earth. There lies, we believe, the very responsibility of poets as well as the mission of poetry in large.

For the sake of our responsibility, for the mission of this vital human art, we will keep up our warm entreaties with the Muses relentlessly. Never forsake us. Give us inspiration and render us vulnerable to your charm so that here and now, in face of the holy Lake Koknore (Qinghai lake), we resolve and pray:

Let Mother Nature be deeply revered. Let life in all shapes loose and free. Let civilization be held in genuine sanctity. And finally let poetry retake root in human hearts.

山地族群的生存记忆与被拯救中的边缘影像

——在 2014 中国（青海）世界山地纪录片节圆桌会议上的发言

我一直有这样一个看法，或许这个看法在有的人看来并不成立，但我至今仍然坚持我的这种看法，那就是人类的文明有两大系统，简单地说就是海洋文明和山地文明，当然，在这里我说的是两大最主要的文明系统，不可否认，在人类的文明传承中，经过数以千年历史的变化，我们人类在今天，还能看见这样一个现象并未改变。海洋文明的传承，最终伴随着人类的探险、贸易、迁徙、掠夺、殖民等活动，致使这一文明的影响日益扩大。特别是在近五百年来，由于人类航海技术的不断提升，海洋文明的传播，就其传播速度和覆盖面而言，毫无疑问大大地超过了其他的文明。

我要告诉大家的是，我在这里说的海洋文明，完全是相对于山地文明而言的，我没有用诸如西方文明、印度文明、阿拉伯文明、中国文明等等这样一些概念。同样在此，我无意去研究和探讨，在海洋文明的传播过程中，甚至不止一次出现过的，这两种文明之间所形成的冲突。更为严重的是，这一冲突曾导致一些古老的文明开始衰落和消亡。无可讳言，拉丁美洲和非洲等地域古老文明所遭遇过的危险，并最终酿成悲剧，原因就来自于这种冲突。难怪在纪念哥伦布发现美洲大陆五百年的

Existential Memory of Mountain Inhabitants and Marginalized Images Coming to the Rescue

Key-note Address at the 2014 Roundtable Forum of

Qinghai World Mountain Documentary Festival

A supposition I have been increasingly coming under the spell of, which to much frankly personal bias, totally untenable, is this: human civilizations to date fall into two typologies, i. e. maritime and mountainous. My dissenting views, of course, could be set forth or elaborated in more logical terms to avoid the blurs and distortions which ensue necessarily in such flagrant reductionist generalities. Wherever the truth may lie, the fact looks to me crystal clear: the so called human civilization is the sum total of the increased productivity and opulence by and for the evolving man and the spiritual fruits achieved which offers both an interpretation of the natural world around him as well as a consecration of his daily work and his relationship with fellow beings and higher beings. Given the inherent dynamism materialized in expansionist adventures, trading, colonies, massive exodus and immigration, gunboats pillage and plunder, the contributions and historical significance of the maritime civilization, pioneered by the Greco- Roman people and succeeded by the Germanic- Slavic races, stand out clearly and overwhelmingly. A hard and stern look at the world history since 1500, due to the superior technology, especially in armaments and naval shipbuilding/ navigation, which facilitated the diffusion of the Greco- Roman model to outperform and dwarf almost the majority on the face of the earth, confirms the maritime supremacy beyond doubt.

Here I deliberately oppose maritime civilization to mountainous civilization without positing the dichotomy between western civilization and non- western variants such as Arabic/ Indus or Chinese, not unmindful of the unfortunate rivalries between the domination of the former and the subjugation of the latter as well as their deleterious effects. The result was, due to the emergence of the maritime races enjoying the mobility and superiority on the oceans of the

时候，美洲土著人民（包括美洲后来形成的混血人种），他们的态度就与纪念活动的主办者们截然不同，他们发出的是几百年来被压抑了的抗议的声音。

在此，我需要声明，我不是在这里来赘述，这一冲突产生的背景和过程，而是想要说明，海洋文明作为一个庞大的文明体系，无论你对它进行何种的评价，它都是一个我们必须面对的现实存在。需要再声明的是，我在这里所指的海洋文明，是从更广义的角度来看的，是指这一文明的产生和传播，都与海洋密切相关，更确切地说，这是自始至终相对于山地文明来谈的。否则，会发生传统意义上对世界现存几大文明的误读。只有这样，我们才会从另一极，来为古老而伟大的山地文明定位。我讲以上这些，只有一个目的，那就是要为我阐释清楚，山地文明的重要性，做一个必不可少的铺垫，仅此而已。

可能大家都已经注意到了，我今天发言用的题目，就是此次论坛的主题，"山地族群的生存记忆与被拯救中的边缘影像"，其实这并非是我的冒昧自大，我更不愿意给大家造成这样的印象，我在给这样一个论坛主题作结论性的总结，其实我的这一席话与在座的各位一样，仅仅是一家之言。因为我知道，围绕着这样一个主题，每一个人的发言都会从不同的角度，表达出自己独有的观点，而这些鲜明的思想，都将成为我们这次论坛，最具有建设性的贡献，也正因为大家的共同参与，这样一个各抒己见的对话，才富有更加积极的意义。

现在我必须把谈话的内容，拉回到"山地文明"这样一个中心。不知道，大家注意到这样一个现象没有：近一两百年来的社会变革和经济发展，在全世界范围内，经济和社会发育程度最高的地方，似乎都在不同国家的沿海地带，或者说许多国家经济最繁荣的区域，大都在海岸线

world, a major alteration in the configuration of world affairs at the expense of many old centers of civilization in Africa and Latin America. What is truly significant in the perspective of Stavrianosian world history is the Iberian crusading impulse, initiated by a handful of Spanish swashbuckling conquistadors and mercenaries, turns out to be an operation of global import - the ultimate tragic demise of Mayan and Aztec cultures. No wonder on the 500th anniversary in celebration of Columbus's discovery of the New World, the Spaniards and the Hispanic world were sharply divided, a voice of dissent suppressed for centuries on behalf of the aborigines by he natives and Creoles included.

Here I must omit, due to the limited time at my disposal, a survey of the nature of such fateful encounters before presenting my core thesis today, that is, given its size and weight, maritime civilization constitutes the overriding status quo we are living with, despite its failings and weaknesses. It should be cautioned again I am making some generalities and that my point is although maritime civilization prevails, mountainous civilization must not be dismissed as out of date or fossilized or retarded.

Each in the audience today must have wondered what today's topic, i. e. "Existential Memory of Mountain Inhabitants and Marginalized Images Coming to the Rescue" really implies. A topic as such bespeaks of something like political correctness undeniably. But still, I ascend the podium, humbled and honored by the attendance of such a team of esteemed experts and professionals and I do anticipate and appeal to you to air your views and speak your minds heedless of what the topic might frown upon. Cross fertilization of minds, as befits the occasion, is meaningful only when arguments are offered and countered, given and taken.

I must curb the impulse of digression to focus on the corollary concept of maritime civilization, which is, mountain civilization. As we all know, the material culture of mankind has changed more in the past hundred years than it did in the previous five thousand years. The name of the game for this epochal transformation is the Industrial Revolution during the 1780s when a breakthrough, of prime importance for modern world, did occur in economic productivity as it provided the economic and military basis for the hegemony of maritime civilization, a goal aspired to by most of the underdeveloped countries.

的附近。而恰恰相反，许多国家较为封闭、落后和贫困的区域，大多集中在高原和山地，这些地方往往交通不便，有的甚至置身于大陆腹地的最深处。无论从今天社会学和人类学的角度来观察，"山地文明"所保持着的原生态性，以及这种古老文明所具有的文化特质，其珍贵程度，对于当下人类来说都是无法估量的，它的价值将随着人类对自身的深度认识，越发显现出来。任何事物，永远有着它的两面性，由于"山地文明"这样一种特殊的处境，千百年来生活在高原和山地的不同族群，他们才有幸和不幸地延续着自己古老的历史，他们独特的宇宙观、价值观、生活方式才在历史的选择中得以幸存。说他们有幸，那是因为这种文化延续，一直没有被外来的力量完全中断，他们已经成为这个世界多元文化的重要组成部分；说他们不幸，那是因为，他们那不可被替代的哲学思想、思维习惯、文化传统等等，正在被力量完全不对称的，外来的强势文化所包围和消解。

但始终令人欣慰的是，直到今天，虽然面临种种的威胁和危险，许多族群仍顽强地坚守着自己的文化传统，保留着自己的语言和文字，毫无疑问，这些濒临灭亡的语言和文字，在当今仍然是记录这些族群生存记忆的工具。正因为这些古老的文化还被传承着，它就像一种声音，虽然依稀弱小，却在人类进入二十一世纪的时候，再一次唤醒了人类已经沉睡的良知。特别是在今天还在不断加速的全球化时代，理性权力的滥用肆无忌惮，尤其是新自由主义重商文化，对全球弱势族群的冲击，已经到了最严重的地步，其造成的灾难性后果，已经摆在了我们面前。

据说，在今天一些弱势族群的语言和文字的消亡，其速度之快令人震惊。当然，就是在这样一个危机四伏的时候，我们才越发感觉到，要保护好不同民族的文化传统，这个世界留给我们的时间已经不多。"山

A phenomenon, for everyone with the naked eye to see, is that the world's most favored regions, in terms of economic prosperity and social opulence, are either coastal or interior close to the coast. In stark contrast, mountains and upland areas remain invariably economic backwater due to physical isolation and inaccessibility to the economic sustenance and intellectual stimulation from outside. This sounds paradoxical, but it is commonly assumed, that isolated and backward mountains, from the latest thinking of contemporary anthropology and ethnography, contains qualities in the residues of aboriginal and pristine cultures, valuable and priceless for a better understanding of our past and as studies of human nature.

In this sense, mountains and uplands shorn of economy take off are a blessing in disguise. Mountain inhabitants are fortunate as physical isolation makes it possible to retain intact their old ways, value systems and world views, surviving the iron law of postal- Neolithic mutation and natural selection, becoming incorporated into the overall splendid cultural legacy and to which all races and peoples claim. On the other hand, mountain people, in face of the growing complexity of modern society, are in jeopardy, threatening to be overrun and engulfed by mainstream cultures, lost inexorably to the sway of hegemonic philosophic patterns and cultural traditions.

One thing reassuring is that many traditional societies still cling hard to their old ways of life, time- honored mores and customs, ancient scripts and characters amidst menaces and encroachments approaching thick and fast. Their scripts and characters, although on the brink of extinction, are still used as tool to perpetuate the existential memory, a road sign to a living culture of antiquity, a voice, however muffled, serving its due but dignified role of awakening human conscience that slumbers for too long. In a world where globalization proceeds apace like wild fire, the rule of reason is usurped and the impact of neo mercantilism falls mainly on the weak cultures and impoverished populace with devastating consequences.

At present, we are aware of a daily basis of the alarming loss throughout the world. One or two languages which abodes absolutely ill for mankind. An old language dies out, so does an old race, because the culture encoded in that language disappears. As such, it entails in essence a human loss and the knell of mankind. The cultural "genes" encoded in mountain

地文明"中留存的"基因"和"密码",或许现在已经成了我们人类必需进行抢救的最后的"记忆库",这绝不是我在危言耸听。

我不能在这里推断,如果今天的人类,失去了对过去的记忆,人类是否还能真正地认识自己。这种集体的失忆,是无论如何不敢去想象的。在今天,用影像记录的方式,当然这仅仅是一种方式,来拯救和记录我们的"山地文明",已经被大家所共识,这一共识在不同的国家和组织,其实已经变成了广泛的行动。最为可贵的是,有不少形形色色,数以十万计纪录片机构,当然也包括那些纪录片独立制作人,在这一领域,做出的贡献是极为非凡的。我们应该向他们表示敬意。他们的不凡之举和敬业精神,是人类能够相信自己,并能够把自己的昨天、今天和明天联系在一起的关键所在。

尽管是这样,今天我们还是要继续呼吁和倡导,对山地族群的生存状况,再进行全方位的、准确的、真实的记录。我想这些被拯救一般记录下来的影像,除了具有重要的史料意义外,还会让人类在认识自己昨天的同时,真正理性地找到通往明天的道路。这条道路将更合乎人的全面发展,更具有人道的精神,更兼顾公平和正义。如果没有人类的历史,就一定不会有人类的未来,我以为,这就是我们要举办山地纪录片节的最重要的也是最直接的原因,这也是影像记录"山地文明"的价值所在。

civilizations might be the last pool of existential memory of not only mountain residents but also of us urban dwellers to be salvaged and conserved before it is too late.

In this world of dazzling movement, thronged as never before with so many cars and pedestrians bustling and hustling on the sidewalks and city streets, blocking each other's passage, I dare not brood over the macabre prospects of us humans in fidgeting seclusion of high apartment buildings, unable to take stock of ourselves owing to a loss of reminiscence and remembrance of our past. That is why each of you in the audience is bestirred to the rescue of mountain civilizations stranded with the means you excel - the superb tool of imaging . So in the name of camera, we are summoned and gathered under the glorious standard of saving the mountains, and you, under various covers, auspices, individual documentary artists, independent producers, professional agencies, all have a vital role to play deserving our regards and salutations of the highest order. Note your professionalism and devoted industry will prove the key linking us with our past, present and future.

I, for one, will continue to clamor for the widest attention on the deplorable state of mountain civilizations and to urge for a fuller, more comprehensive and more authentic recording of what happens under our very noses in the mountains and uplands. These footages and images, aside their historical function, will supply rich food for a better awareness of our past as well as rational clues to point to a more enlightened future, a future wherein humans will evolve in a more humanistic, harmonious and all rounded way, a future wherein justice and equality will prevail simply because man deprived of his past is without tomorrow. Hence our forum here today as a ritual to renew our sense of mission and arouse each other to the level of intellectual and emotional intensity necessary to venture into the wilderness and mountains.

向诗歌致敬

——在 2014 国际诗人帐篷圆桌会议上的致辞

我亲爱的各位诗人同行，各位尊敬的朋友：

本届国际诗人帐篷圆桌会议，在大家的共同努力下，已经顺利地完成了各项议程，今晚就要圆满闭幕了。我想此时此刻，大家都有一个共同的感受，那就是每一次诗人的聚会，就如同在完成一种庄严、古老、崇高的仪式，为此，我敢肯定在人类所有的艺术形式中，唯有诗歌并与之相伴随生发出来的音乐和舞蹈，才会产生这样一种不同凡响、更为彰显生命本质的行为和力量。

在这里，我不由得想到了伟大的西班牙诗人加西亚·洛尔加，他始终认为，通过有生命的媒介和联系传达诗的信息，最能发挥诗歌中"杜恩德"（duende）的作用，如果直接翻译成中文就是"灵魔的力量"。是的，我坚信每一位真正的诗人，都具有这样一种上天赋予他的神奇力量。恐怕这也是数千年来，诗歌充满灵性和魅力，而又经久不衰的重要理由，同样这也是人类热爱诗歌，并把诗歌视为自己精神生活中最为美好、最为温暖、最为动人那样一个部分的真正原因。

永恒的时间和人类的心灵渴望，已经无数次地证明过，诗歌的存在，无疑是人类不断延续个体生命和集体生命的实证，因为它从生命存在更为本质的角度，强调了诗歌在精神世界中的作用，也正是这种对精神的需求和向往，才让人类与别的动物产生了更大的区别。从这个意义

A Tribute to Poetry

A Speech Given at the Poetic Evening
Dedicated to Humanity of the Tent Roundtable Forum of World Poets

Dear Fellow Poets, respectable friends:

At last, this latest edition of our poetry festival associated with the most beautiful lake of China, this biennial signal event attended by such a prestigious bevy of key figures of contemporary poetic writing, home and a-broad, has realized, under the theme of " Poetic Writing in the Poet and the Poet in Society", all the set agendas as we are now led to the point at which to call it a day. This moment and over here, I trust a sacred, ancient and sublime sense of ritual must overwhelm this crowd of us that daily live in celebration of life. The wondrous work achieved by poetry reminds me of an ultimate fact that only poetry, among all forms of human art, with all its attendant dance and music, can reinstate the wholeness of life in a way nothing else can.

This calls my remembrance to the admirable buzz word "duende" invented by Garcia Lorca, the great Andalucian bard who trusts "duende", the magical power, can only be detonated, like nuclear fission, by good poetry which involves delving into the subconscious to mine some substance that will transform this world. Yes, I firmly trust each poet in the company of this evening is endowed by the Creator with the Lorcan duende, thanks to which we have been, since time immemorial, avid of Truth, not lies, of the Good, not of evil, of the Beauty, not of the Ugly. The secret of poetry's lasting popularity, i. e. people have kept returning to poetry and reserving an important place in their spiritual life, lies precisely in this poets' almost self- indulgent infatuation with their calling.

The infinitude of time and the profundity of human cravings are eternal testament to the essentiality of poetry for the preservation and proliferation of humanity, individual or collective, at the level of either physical or spiritual. It has been our most recalcitrant act of faith that man cannot live by bread alone.

上而言，只要人类的生命存在并把这种对精神的需求不断延续下去，那么诗歌就永远不会离开我们！

朋友们，诗歌就像一束熊熊燃烧的火把，直到今天它仍然站在人类前行的最前列，它照亮了不同种族和人类迈向明天的道路。在曙光开始升起在地平线的时候，诗歌不仅仅是黎明时的号角，它还会给我们一个又一个未卜先知的启示，并随时谦恭地为前行者擦亮眼睛，诗歌既是反抗一切异化的工具，更重要的是它会让人类重新从摇篮中苏醒，再一次认清生命的意义，并辨明人类正确、光明的前进方向！

在这个圆桌会议即将拉上帷幕的时候，请允许我代表在座的各位并以我所居住和生活的这个高原的名义，向我们尊敬的诗人法伊夫·博纳富瓦、尼卡诺尔·帕拉、塔杜施·鲁热维奇、加里·斯奈德、特朗斯特罗姆、郑玲、埃内斯托·卡德纳尔致敬！他们由于年迈和身体的原因，我们不能如愿地邀请他们来到这里，但他们的存在，却时时刻刻给我们坚守诗的梦想，提供了无穷的勇气和力量。我们会从他们的诗歌中，再一次感受到对生命的热爱、对自由的向往、对弱者的同情、对暴力的反抗、对悲伤的抚慰以及对现实永不妥协的追问！

在这里，我还要借此机会，向生活在这个地球上，不同地域、不同民族、不同国家的所有诗人致敬！同样，因为你们的存在，这个充满和并存着进步与危机、幸福与灾难、创造与毁灭的世界，才会让上苍的天平朝着更加和平、正义和美好的方面倾斜！

朋友们，我不得不说"再见"这个词了，我热切地期待着与大家的下一次再见！谢谢你们！谢谢！

The spiritual primacy, nay, indeed, the poetic primacy of man has been touchstone by which man is distinguished from all other species on earth.

Friends, poetry, the beacon light of mankind, forever in the vanguard of human progress, has radiated its warmth and inspiration upon the pathway of world peoples ahead. In the first glimmer of dawn, it serves a clarion call to begin the day's toiling, the oracle to be divined into the mystery of the future, the tool to combat alienation as well as the balm for our agonized hearts. To crown it all, it will awaken the souls that slumber into the significance of life afresh and put us onto the right track again.

Now, at the time of the most symbolic curtain fall, please allow me, on behalf of each of us present and of the Plateau I have made home, to pay tribute to Yves Bonnefoy, Nicanor Parra, Tadeusz Róewicz, Gary Snyder, Tomas Transtromer, Zheng Ling, Ernesto Cardenal. These veterans' marked absence from this festival due to failing health or seniority is sorely regretted, but their lifelong clinging to the poetic dreams has been a perennial source of zeal and strengthen. For their exemplary passion for poetry has brought to light the enormous potential of us younger generation to demonstrate love for life, longing for freedom, sympathy for the weak and downtrodden, to oppose barbarity, to console those in affliction and adversity, and last but not in the least, to enact a dialogue with reality unflinchingly, because ultimately " the options of life, justice, dignity and beauty, amply represented by poetry, are the only alternative left to us humans", an enterprise worthy of our lasting human name.

Once more, cap in hand, let me rise and salute all our fellow poets across the globe. Emphatically due to your presence and involvement in a world full of promise and crisis, bliss and woe, creation and destruction, the pendulum of the Providence swings in human favor of peace, justice and beauty.

Friends, though mostly reluctant to say the word, I must face the music and utter adieu to you all. And this certainly makes the best excuse for your next visit. Thank you for your attention.

诗歌的本土写作和边缘的声音

——在 2014 青海国际诗人帐篷圆桌会议上的演讲

当我用这样一个题目开始演讲的时候，我首先想到的是，在今天这样一个新自由主义思潮和资本逻辑横行的时代，我们不同民族的文化，确实已经遭到了从未有过的威胁。所谓新自由主义的思想和主张，之所以能大行其道，那是因为不断加速的全球化进程，给他们提供了自认为最实在的佐证，同样也因为这样一个全球化的过程，新自由主义思想和主张，才找到了似乎谁也无法阻挡的传播空间。

其实，所谓"全球化"，就是资本的主要操控者，让资本按照其意愿自由地流动，或者说让经济和金融打破原有的国家和区域的经济界限，并使之整合为一。这种被称为世界经济场的状态，实际上是这个世界经济竞争游戏规则的制定者们，他们强行而巧妙地带着大家玩的一场，永远只有利于他们的游戏。

我们知道的国际货币基金组织和世界贸易组织，当然也包括像世界银行这样的面向全球的机构，不言而喻，就是他们在背后用一双看不见的手，操控着的一系列跨国组织。在当下，让我们感到这种威胁越来越严重是，这种资本的自由入侵，以及它所带来的只为疯狂营利的唯一市场逻辑，已经给我们的文化传承和发展，造成了极为不利的影响。

需要声明的是，我并不反对市场对经济的主要调节作用，而是反对新自由主义的荒谬主张，这种主张有时并不是明目张胆的，它们还常常穿着虚假的外衣，以经济的高速增长为诱饵，强势美化资本的自由流动带来的所谓种种好处。它们只强调经济增长在人类生活中的唯一性，只把单一的经济指标的提高，作为社会发展的整体的终极目标。

Localized Poetic Writing and marginalized Voice

Key- note Speech Delivered at the Opening Ceremony of

2014 Tent Roundtable Forum of World Poets

The topic for today brings me instantly to the nexus of events set off by the ascendancy of neo - laissez - faireism and the spread of crass capitalism and attendant threats caused to cultural, ecological and ethnic diversity. The pulverizing effects in the wake of the rapid integration of neo- laissez- faire philosophy and the swift globalization, to the market fundamentalists, are a hard case of self- fulfilling prophecy. No wonder they herald a newly emerging flattening world in which their iron hearted advocacy takes a firm hold on popular imagination.

By globalization, as a provocative turn of phrase, in fact, is taken a general trend that capital barons masquerading as transnational businesses move to globalize the world by rapidly dissolving the social and economic barriers between nations and transforming the world's diverse populations into a blandly uniform market. This is a game played adroitly by the market fundamentalists who define the rules to enrich the rich at the expense of workers, the environment, the traditional values.

The so called flattening of the world, more or less, is a virtual reality created by invisible but omnipotent forces, of which, inadvertently, super world bodies like WTO, IMF, who claim to be amoral transnational guardian of public good, are major players as an invisible hand in tearing apart our world instead of guiding it and keeping it from going off the rails. Increasingly, our former warm, cozy, thriving local communities, industries, and cultures are crowded out. Such disempowering dangers must not be underestimated.

It should be cautioned from the very outset I am not mindless of the legitimate regulating function of the market in economy. Our job is certainly not to trash the market but to give its defenders on the far Right their due: market fundamentalists invariably hold the social good is best served by allowing people to pursue their self interest without any thought of the Good, the True and Beauty. Such advocacy in favor of uninhibited flow of fund, often assuming the disarmingly deceptive and beguilingly innocent mantle, is at best a perversion of human nature, no matter how much tangible and quick benefits in form of rapid GDP ratio it can deliver. The overall goal of mankind must be reconciled with purely mercantile necessities.

由于这种主张，在社会生活中人的全面发展的理念，被资本形成的权力统治曲解，一些本应该由国家和政府去服务的公共领域，也开始大面积地倒退，一些新的社会问题的形成，包括失业和贫困人口的增加，社会福利的减少，可以说从根本上讲，这种所谓全球化的资本主义，给人类带来的恶果已经显而易见，它让许多国家和政府的社会功能大大减弱，甚至让一些政府在社会保障、教育、卫生、文化等方面的服务变成了缺席者。

这种可怕的利益逻辑，既抹杀了文化的特性，同时又让我们生产的文化产品，开始同质化和趋同化。在这方面我们有许多例证，比如对好莱坞电影生产模式的追捧，就使不少国家的民族电影业遭到了毁灭性的打击，这种情况在第三世界国家中尤为严重。一味要求票房的价值，已经成为衡量其作品价值的一个可怕的标准，这种商业化泛滥的情形，对真正有价值的文化发展，所造成的损害，超过了历史上的任何一个时期。

在许多国家和地区，对传统的非物质文化的保护和发展，原有的许多补贴也被降到了最低。许多国家和地区，毫无秩序地过度地开发旅游，对本应该保护的原生态文化，也进行了破坏性的商业利用。最让人不可接受的是，这种与灾难完全可以划等号的经济文化模式，却在必须尊重市场规律的幌子下，被许多新自由主义的宣教者，拿到无数国家去兜售，并在这些国家建立起了自己的"商业"文化王国，其结果只能

Such logic of globalization, to say the least, is lopsided. Perversion of human nature leads to intentional mis- defining of the obligations of the government to the extent many public goods, which traditionally fall into the administrative scope, is nobody's business. Many nation states have withdrawn en masse from sectors of public goods. Many people, particularly in less developed countries, have been hurt absent being bailed out by a social security net. New social problems crop up. Unemployment is rife. Fringe benefits and welfare become scarce. This is not progress, but regress. If globalization is only about the spread of crass capitalism, indeed it has become increasingly clear the dangers inherent in the philosophy of neo laissez faire has materialized to the detriment of the fulfillment of administrative functions of many an absenteeing nation states and governments .

This naturally triggers a backlash and complaint against globalization. We are living in a world of manufactured needs, mass consumption and mass infotainment, motivated by profits and driven by the aggregate preferences of billions of consumers. Belonging by default to this global village, people emulate and toady to the Hollywood model and churn out MacDonaldized movies and soap series to the extent cultural products outside USA all have an American look and take an American outlook. Movies industry particularly falls a prey to the Mammon of "box value" in many third world countries wherein what counts boils down to blatant profiteering motives. Therefore harms done to cultural diversity is unmatched and unprecedented in the annals of mankind due to such heedless pursuit of profit, let alone the environment and other social values being either compromised or marginalized.

The development of our political arrangements has not kept pace with the development of cultural production. There is the uneven misallocation of resources between private goods and public goods obvious for anyone with the naked eye to see. In many developing countries, enthusiasm and subsidies for the production and protection of the intangible assets wane and dwindle to a record low. Over exploitation of hot scenic spots and enchanting sights, many being of un - spoilt and aboriginal character, deserving maximum degree of conservation, has been taken for granted. What abhors me most is such calamitous modes of development are everywhere exalted to the sky by neo laissez faire preachers in collaboration with various imposters and money chasers to forge their kingdoms of profit ostensibly in the name of incubating culture. Indeed, unless serious steps are taken to readdress the flagrant wrong to conserve the environment and strengthen cultures- this "juggernaut of globalization as

是，那些被传承了数千年的地域文化，不同民族的语言、文字以及独特的生活方式，都无不面临着死亡和消失的考验。

除了这些，新干涉主义带来的诸多问题，也在这个地球的四面八方开始显现。在中东，特别是在伊拉克、埃及等地，战火不断，在原有的政治社会秩序被破坏之后，新的政治社会秩序并没有真正地建立起来。

由此，我们不会不去深层地思考，不同文明、不同价值体系、不同宗教信仰、不同文化背景的国家和民族，如何由自己去选择和建立更合乎自己的社会制度以及发展道路，如何更好地为建立一个更加和平的世界而开展积极的建设性的对话。

面对这样一个世界，为什么我要如此坚持和强调诗歌的本土写作呢？其实，我上面的发言已经说明了很多问题，这也是我为什么要反对新自由主义的一个根本原因。当然，无可讳言，我是站在全球范围这样一个角度来讲的。作为生活在地球村里的一个诗人，我想无论我们生活在这个世界的哪一个区域，我们捍卫人类伟大文明成果的神圣职责，是永远不可放弃的。从人类道德的高度而言，尤其在今天，当这种珍贵文明的基础，在被"全球化"动摇的时候，我们只能选择挺身而出，而不能袖手旁观。不过需要进一步阐释的是，我所主张的本土写作，是相对于这个世界更大范围而言的，是对新自由主义"全球化"思潮的一种在理论上的反动。

因为"全球化"在文化上的一个最大特征，就是抹杀个性，就是让多样性变成单一性，让差异性变成同一性，使这个世界多声部的合唱，最终变成一个声音。更为恐怖的是，这种由跨国资本控制和自由市场所形成的力量，毫无疑问对文化多样性的危害，是最为致命的，这绝不是我危言耸听，在亚洲，在非洲，在拉丁美洲，这样的例子层出不穷，乌拉圭著名作家爱德华多·加莱亚诺的《拥抱之书》，就深刻地揭示了这一问题的本质。

Americanization", in just a few decades, will eradicate the cultural, ecological and even zoological diversity that took millions of years of human, plant and animal evolution to produce.

On top of these hazards, neo laissez faire advocates have created more problems than solved. Especially in the Middle East, the triumphant collapse of strongmen like Saddam Hussein and Mubarak has brought neither economic stability nor social democracy to former Iraq and Egypt, or for that matter, to the rest of the world.

Such disheartening massive geopolitical disorder inclines us to rethink this global crisis has to be overcome if humanity is to assert command over its destiny. The point of departure for such self assertion must be revelation that human history is too complex to be predesigned according to a banal reductionist hypothesis of humans, regardless of religion, ethnicity, origin of civilization, value system, all factors to be taken into consideration before engaging in a constructive dialogue for a more humane and peaceful world.

Living in a "gilded age" and a globe out of control, why should I cling so hard to the stance of a poetry steeped in the native soil? The above vehement tirade against the excessive reliance on the market mechanism and the shortcomings of neo liberalism provides clues into my way of thinking. I am, of course, generalizing on the global level as a poet. There is no shirking the moral responsibility, wherever we happen to be, of protecting and defending the sanctity of all the spiritual fruits and enriching the cultural cornucopia of mankind. From a moral vantage when the forces of globalization begin to erode the very basis of civilization and sap its vitality, we poets must rise to the occasion to magnify the capacity of individuals and inscribe them on the world with the means we excel, which is, poetic writing per se. Here a word must be in place to qualify my position that localized poetic writing be used as an anti- homogenizing force, an antidote against the potential threats posed by the variant of globalization promoted by neo liberalism or market fundamentalists.

In cultural terms, globalization tends towards homogenization and erasing of personality and particularity into sameness and identity, solo into chorus, as the most salient feature. In every way this should be taken as both prognosis and diagnosis: the forces of globalization, a coalition of transnational businesses and jungle market, are sworn foes to cultural diversity. This urgent warning about the state of global cultures should not fall on deaf ears of world poets, the truth of which is poignantly illuminated in the *El libro de los abrazos* by Uruguayan Eduardo Galeano, one of our age's sages.

While worries about the negative outcome of globalization are legitimate,

在这里，需要说明的是，我不是在探讨一般意义上的人类在发展中存在的问题，更不是要否定人类在工业文明和科技进步方面所取得的巨大成就。我想要表述的是，这个世界上的任何一种文化，哪怕是最弱势的文化，它也有无可辩驳的独立存在的价值。但是，令我们感到不安的是，今天的市场逻辑只要求文化产品的商业价值，而把许多具有精神价值的文化产品弃之一旁。诗歌的本土写作，说到底就是要求诗人在任何时候，都应该成为自己所代表的文化符号，都应该义无反顾地代表这个文化发出自己必须发出的声音。诗人被称为诗人，据我所知，这个称号从来就不是一个职业的称谓，而这一称号却是一个人所共知的社会角色，从某种角度来讲，就如同但丁对于意大利，普希金对于俄罗斯，密茨凯维奇对于波兰，叶芝对于爱尔兰，诗人在更长的历史时空中，承担的社会角色，毫无疑问就是他的祖国文化的第一代言人，同样也是他的民族的无可争议的良心。

在这个消费至上和物质主义的时代，或许已经有不少人，开始怀疑诗人在今天存在的价值，对此不用担心，因为只要有人类存在，人类伟大的文明的延续就不会停止，而作为人类文明最重要的精神支柱之一的诗歌，就不会丧失其崇高的地位和作用。

在当今这个让人类处于极端困惑，并正在遭遇深度异化的现实世界里，诗歌除了其固有的审美作用，以及用词语所创造的无与伦比的人类精神高度外，已经勇敢地承担起了捍卫人类伟大文明的重任，已经成为反抗一切异化和强权的工具。我们一定要清醒地看到，今天的诗歌写作，已经不仅仅是诗人的个体活动，当面对强大的经济世界主义和国际经济强权的压迫时，一个世界性的诗歌运动，正在这个地球的许多地方开展起来，而这一诗歌运动本身，正以其独特的方式，去抚慰生活在不同地域的人们的心灵，并用诗歌点燃的火炬去引领人类走向一个更符合人的全面发展的新的理想目标。这个目标不是别的，它会让人类再一次相信，这个由诗歌构建的精神高地，就是通往明天的真正的乌托邦！

and indeed very important, it must be conceded, ignoring the ability of the industrial and technological advances to empower humans misses their historically positive role-playing on human freedom and happiness. My point here is that any culture, however small and weak, deserves a place to be sustained. What I argue against is the logic of ultra right market which demands cultural products, no matter how much spiritual value they embody and contain, unless they sell hot, will be thrust forth to scorn and scattered to the four winds. When I am talking of localized poetic writing, I mean a poet should make himself a civic voice, a mouthpiece of popular content and discontent, an icon of his own people, speak unabashedly and unflinchingly to the world and for the world. To the best of my knowledge, poetry is never a vocation, a line of business like carpentry and a poet is never a careerist a blacksmith is. Yet each ancient and great civilization accords a poet an esteemed status, one commonly agreed upon and respected. Their place and importance in the spiritual life of mankind shall not be challenged. In a sense, in the firmament of world poetry, Dante to Italy, Pushkin to Russia, Mickiewicz to Poland, Yeats to Ireland, (what a cluster of lyrical talent!) are all meant to be the spokesmen of their culture, the conscience of his their folks beyond dispute.

Consumerist capitalism, which reigns supreme across the globe, does not tend towards cultural harvest and spiritual plenty. Rumors and doubts are rampant about the sweet uses of poetry . I for one, stand firm in the belief no decent society can function properly without some role reserved for poets, simply because poetry is one of the most important pillars to buttress the spirituality of its people.

We are living in a world fraught with spiritual doldrums and fragmented mentality that brings matters to a head. It is not enough to roll in wealth and bask in creature which comfort all kinds of technical gadgetry supplies. People also need an aesthetic vision of a better future. Poets have in the past crystallized admirably what common people widely sensed but vaguely vocalized ideas about the justification of civilization and the dignity of man as antidote against alienation and hegemony. Let us be clear about our mission today: a world poetry movement on the rise meets head-on the supremacy of globalization that threatens to homogenize everything and engulf the civic society. Poets, attentive to the aftermath of history per se, afire with passion for justice and freedom, follow the suit of their worthy predecessors, come to the rescue and solace of people in spiritualized torment and disarray and hoist the torches of poetry ascending the heights of light and sweetness, built upon the solid rock of enlightened human Intellect which leads into the palaces of Utopia of tomorrow.

诗歌是人类迈向明天最乐观的理由

——在 2015 青海湖国际诗歌节开幕式上的致辞

尊敬的郝鹏省长、尊敬的各位诗人、女士们、先生们、朋友们：

在这里，我首先要说的是，因为在座诸位热情的参与和努力，今天我们才能如期相聚在这个地球上最令人向往的高地——青藏高原，毫无疑问，这是一件值得我们庆贺并将永远珍藏在记忆中的事，朋友们，此时此刻，我们为什么不能用热烈的掌声来为我们这样一次伟大的聚会而喝彩呢？当然，作为东道主，请允许我代表中国作家协会和本届国际诗歌节组委会，向来自世界各地的诗人朋友们表示最热忱的欢迎，同时还要向为本届诗歌节的主办付出了辛勤劳动并贡献了聪明和智慧的各相关机构表示最衷心的感谢！

是的，朋友们，我们是因为诗歌，才从这个世界的四面八方来到这里，同样是因为诗歌，我们才能把人类用不同语言和文字创造的奇迹，再一次汇聚在这里，完全可以肯定，这是诗歌的又一次胜利！当然，诸位，在这里我不能简单地把我们的相聚，归结为诗歌之神对我们的一次眷顾，如果真的是那样的话，作为一个有着责任感和人类情怀的诗人，那将是我们对诗歌所具有的崇高价值和重要作用的极大不敬。

朋友们，事实证明，这个世界直到今天还需要诗歌，因为物质和技术，永远不可能在人类精神的疆域里，真正盛开出馨香扑鼻的花朵，更不可能用它冰冷的抽象数据和异化逻辑，给我们干渴的心灵带来安抚和慰藉。这个世界还需要诗歌，是因为在这个充满着希望与危机、战争与和平、幸福与灾难的现实面前，诗歌就是善和美的化身，正如捷克伟大

Why Poetry Still Matters Today?

A Speech given by Jidi Majia, chairman of Qinghai Lake Intl Poetry Festival, deputy chairman of All China Writers Union

Respected Governor, Mr. Hao Peng, respected fellow poets, ladies, gentlemen and friends:

Thanks to the wonderful organizing work on the part of the Organizing Committee, today, the very fact that this choicest group of poets travelling from all quarters of the earth, summoned to be a part of one of the most spectacular poetic pageantries- Qinghai Lake Intl Poetry Festival, will make us all proudly cherish the five days to come which will celebrate the magical gifts of poets and powers of poetry. Dear Fellow poets, please do not hesitate to give thunderous applauses to this unusual gathering radiant in our collective pride in being poets we are. Doubly as deputy chairman of All China Writers Union and chairman of QLIPF, I must offer my warmest greetings to all the poets home and abroad as well as my hearty gratitude to all the organizing staff.

A victorious experience I must call this pageantry, my friends, with the wondrous essence of rallying around poetic vision, when 120 special men and women, regardless of color or race or language or religion, congregate to witness poetry as a tool to push reform in society and to awaken conscience by opposing war to peace , evil to justice. Do not for a second fancy the Muses care a whit about this cheap vanity who certainly demand us in return for her favor our collective sensitivity and our spiritual height as agents to influence society and effect changes favorable to the promising future of mankind.

Friends, it has been testified and corroborated in world history that this world of ours, this beautiful blue planet humans inhabit, cannot do and go around without poets. By this I simply mean all our technological gadgetry and our internet, marvelous providers of creature comforts and super sustenance albeit, are not enough. Robots don't bloom . Life cannot be governed mechanically

诗人雅罗斯拉夫·塞弗尔特在诗中写的那样,"要知道摇篮的吱嘎声和朴素的催眠曲,还有蜜蜂和蜂房,要远远胜过刺刀和枪弹",他这两句朴实得近似于真理的诗句,实际上说出了这个世界上所有诗人的心声。

我这样说,绝非是痴人说梦,因为就在今天的现实世界,那些正在发生着冲突和杀戮的区域,无辜的平民,正流离失所成为离开故土的难民,当然,同样是在那样一些地方,诗歌却与他们如影相随、不离不弃,他们的诗歌就是怀念故土的谣曲和至死不忘的母语,毫无疑问,他们在内心和灵魂中吟诵的箴言,就是他们最终能存活下去的依靠和勇气,诗歌和语言在这样的特定环境中,也已经成了反对一切暴力和压迫的最后的武器。

这个世界还需要诗歌,是因为诗歌既是属于更多的极少数,同时它又从未丧失过大众的认知和喜爱,或许诗歌的奇妙就在这里,因为我们不知道还有哪一种艺术形式,能像诗歌那样既能飞越形而上的天空,伸手去触摸万象的星群,又能匍匐在现实的大地上,去亲吻千千万万劳动者的脚跟。难怪,尼加拉瓜伟大诗人卡德莱尔,在二十年前,就把群众性的诗歌运动与被压迫民族的解放事业联系在了一起。

or solely by reference to the audited accounts of a nation. Cold balance sheets and logic of alienation is no balm for our parched souls. While there is so little optimistic in the way our age is shaping, one of hope mitigated by crisis, peace so fragile as to seem war, happiness at times blighted by catastrophe, we mustn't be deemed preening ourselves too much upon being poets or touting poetry as a substance which transforms awareness and social life. Yes, we do stand for the Kindness and Beauty. Jaroslav Seifert, the eminent Chech poet, writes with such eloquence even when he concentrates on small and intimate gestures :

Aren't the creaking a cradle and the humming of a lullaby,
As well as bees swarming around a beehive,
More congenial a sight than bayonets and canon balls?

Invoking such homely forces as bees and nursery songs as symbols of human needs, Seifert speaks on the behalf of us all.

Don't think I am an obtrusive doomsayer. In this very world of ours, several wars of fratricide have raged on with disheartening tolls of human losses day in and day out. Displaced civilians fall a prey to the wickedness and stupidity of war lords and politicians. Yet in the makeshift huts and functionary refuge camps, their chests heave and resonate with the familiar tunes of their childhood lullaby and the most memorable lines of their best loved national poets in the mother tongues they stick to even in the direst hours and in the harshest alien milieu. No doubt, poems chanted from the bottom of their hearts prove the last buttress against hardship and tyranny.

Poetry still matters today. Although an element of eccentricity or anti- socialness might be present in all poets, good poets, who have achieved heroic statue since the Romantic Movement in the 18th century, have never lost their pull on the civilized populace. It is such a paradox that poetry, unlike any other form of art, is capable of soaring through the celestial vaults of metaphysics to reach out for the starry heavens, while at the same time, crawling on the tough terrain of reality, kisses the feet of myriad of working men and toiling women. No wonder, Ernesto Cardenal , the marvelous Nicaraguan poet, associated poetic movements with the liberation of all oppressed nations even 20 years ago.

这个世界还需要诗歌，是因为在跨国的金融资本，完全控制了全球并成为一种隐形的权力体系，从而让人类的心灵更进一步远离我们曾经亲近过的自然和生命本源，当面对这一被极度的消费主义主导的时代，诗歌精神的复苏已成为必然，诗歌仍然以其作为人类精神殿堂不可动摇的根基之一，发挥着谁也无法替代的作用。

这个世界还需要诗歌，是因为诗歌所包含的全部诗歌精神，实际上是人类区别于别的动物最重要的标志，诗歌实际上成了人类所有心灵生活中最必不可少的要素，我们不能想象，缺少诗意精神的一切人类创造，还会真的有什么重要的价值。人类一直在梦想和追求诗意地栖居，实际上就是在为自身定制、以诗意精神为最高准则的一种生活方式，或者说从更高的角度讲，是一种生命的存在方式。这个世界还需要诗歌，是因为作为人，也可以说作为人类，我们要重返到那个我们最初出发时的地方，也只有诗歌——那古老通灵的语言的火炬，才能让我们辨别出正确的方向，找到通往人类精神故乡的回归之路。

朋友们，尽管我们仍然面临着许多困难，但我们从未丧失过对明天的希望。让我们为生活在今天的人类庆幸吧，因为诗歌直到现在还和我们在一起，因此我有理由坚定地相信，诗歌只要存在一天，人类对美好的未来就充满着期待。谢谢大家！

Poetry is high in demand because in this super age wherein capital barons and financial lords, masquerading as transnational businesses , move to globalize the world by rapidly dissolving the social and economic barriers between nations and transforming the world's diverse populations into a blandly uniform market at the expense of workers, the environment, the traditional values. Such an invisible monster increasingly tears apart our society instead of guiding it and keeping it from going off the rails as consumerist mania alienates us further from origin of nature or source of life fundamental to the sanity of human condition. To counter such disempowering dangers , we poets must rise , with the magnetism of poetic expression, the presence and the representative voice of each poet here in the audience, to the majestic heights of opposing material forces with "soul force" by reawakening the solar spirit of poetry in the crowd and initiating a new socio-cultural renewal across our globe. The magical potential of poetry that fosters such transformation and the vilifying spirit of poets shall not be called into question.

Good poetry always matters because the solar spirit of poetry has always illuminated man's pathway strewn with odds and hazards. Poetry is actually the vital dimension of man as man, the spiritual primacy by which man is set apart from other species. I cannot imagine, what little dosage of value is left in all human-made artifacts, unless inspired by the poetic spirit. While philosophers exhort us to inhabit the earth poetically, they are proposing a recipe for happiness tailored for mankind, the secret of the sweetness of living from a higher vantage point, so to speak. Good poetry is still in demand, because, at the long last, it has become an affirmation of the deeply held longing human longing to return to where we came. Only by upholding the torch of poetry, can we divine the right direction, struggle from darkness to some measure of light and walk the right road back home, back to our spiritual home. At long last, the poem "grows into a praise of what is and what could be on this lump in the skies."

Dear Fellow poets, although we face the difficulties of today, we have never lost our faith in tomorrow. Let us jump for joy of living contemporaneous with such fabulously rich veins of poetry left to us by all great poets, living and dead in the firm belief that poetry is the ultimate justification for mankind that eagerly "after a tomorrow stares".

何为诗人？何为诗？

——2016 西昌邛海"丝绸之路"国际诗歌周开幕式演讲

什么是诗歌的地域性、民族性和世界性？这本身就是一个宏阔而抽象的命题。从一般意义而言，世界上任何一个诗人，他的出生地都在这个地球的某一域，在经度和纬度的某一个点上，从更深处来讲，作为人的出生地抑或是诗人的出生地都是他本人无法选择的。

诗人的民族性与诗人出生时所属的民族有关系，也可以说没有关系，那是因为从最基本的民族性来讲，任何一个诗人从他出生的那一天开始，他后天成长的经历，毫无疑问，在他的身上深深地打下他所属的族群和文化的痕迹。但也可以说某种狭义的民族性和地域性与他没有太直接的关系，那是因为任何一个伟大的诗人，他都必须在精神上和思想上超越这种地域和民族的限制，因为卓越的诗人既是他的民族优秀的儿子，同时也还是人类文明滋养的世界性的公民，因为在他的成长过程中当他面对这个世界的时候，他都会去向所有伟大的诗歌经典学习，这里既包括他所属民族的诗歌经典，当然也包括其他民族的诗歌经典。

诗人的世界性与诗歌的世界性往往是一致的，只有当诗人的作品在深刻地表达了自己内心独一无二的感受，同时他的这种表达无论被翻译成世界上哪一种语言，都能找到热爱他的读者和知音的话，他的诗歌也才具有了世界性的价值。

诗人的或者诗歌作品的地域性、民族性以及世界性，是我们今天应该更加关注的一个话题，特别是在全球化的背景下，诗人的民族性、地域性与世界性似乎形成了一种并不对称的关系，有一点可以肯定，没有

Who Is a Poet? What Is Poetry?

Jidi Majia deputy chairman of All China Writers Association

Address at the Opening Ceremony of Xichang.

Qionghai 2016 Silk Road Intl Poetry Week

In what way do we claim a poet that he is, thrice in senses ethnic, national and universal? On a more general plane, the birth of any poet is a happy confluence or a fortuitous coordinate of longitude and latitude. That is , a poet must be connate with a locale on this blue planet , either as a poet or a human being , and he is here or there in spite of himself.

Yet, although it can be argued that the ethnicity of a poet is purely accidental, he still carries , wherever he happens to be , from the day of his birth, indelible marks and traces of physical breeding and spiritual growth peculiar to his own ethnic community and his own folks. Such connections, however ethnically embedded and tenacious, forbids not his mental development and his artistic expansion. To be really great, he must outgrow and overreach himself beyond such genetic and regional confines to emerge eventually and ultimately, both good son of his own people and model citizen of the world, nurtured and fed upon the best spiritual fruit and blossom of various races collectively called humanity. For a good poet necessarily means a good learner on a rich diet of the "selectest treasuries of the selectest forms of manners and of nature" not only of his own race but also of poetic creations of the highest order authored by people inhabiting remote and different quarters of the same earth.

This is bound to give rise to the approximation of the universality of poethood and the universality of his prosody. For only when a poet renders his unique mindset and imaginations luminous and accessible, for whatever of beautiful, true, and majestic his poems contain about the immortal pageantry of life, to which both his people and indeed all peoples are spectators , especially surviving all the travails of translations into varied languages, will he be deemed a great poet, and his work, true poetry deserving of the epithet of universality.

By implication, my reasoning leads to a tentative conclusion that against the large backdrop of contemporary globalization, the ancient trinity of ethnicity, nationality and universality all combined and embodied in a poet, an attribute taken for granted forages , now has been dissolved and disjointed.

一个诗人不在用一种语言写作,甚至有许多诗人把他所使用的语言称为自己的祖国,尤其是那些离开了自己母语的本土,流落在世界各地的诗人,他所坚守的语言就已经成了他与这个世界发生关系的最后一种方式,甚至是他作为诗人能活下去的最充足的理由。

诗歌的地域性和民族性,很多时候呈现出的是一种表象,但是无可讳言,诗歌从它产生的那一天开始,就无法避免其地域性和民族性。然而地域性和民族性的表达却是千差万别的,历史上无数经典的诗人都给我们树立光辉的榜样,我们不能把所谓的地域性和民族性,与这个世界的普遍性对立起来,那样的地域性和民族性无疑是狭隘的、极端的,真正的诗人可以说都是这种所谓地域性、民族性的敌人,那些饱含爱国主义情愫的诗人,他们的作品不仅仅能唤起本国人民的爱国热情,同样也能让别的国家和民族的读者,为他的真挚情感感动,波兰伟大的诗人密茨凯维奇的诗篇就产生了这样的作用。

地域性和民族性的写作,特别是在那些伟大的诗人写作中,都会以极其卓越的艺术方式呈现,这是一种高品质的地域性和民族性的呈现,或者说是一种更具有独特性的价值和诗性的表达,我们可以从这些诗中,发现它所描述的山脉、河流、岩石、树木、花草以及亘古不变的太阳,都带有一种别样的色彩,我理解这就是一个诗人不同于另一个诗人的价值所在。我阅读英国诗人狄兰·托马斯的时候,就有这样的印象。他诗歌中的英国威尔士就是他带给我们的,一个不同于这个地球上任何一个地方的属于他的文学世界。

在美国二十世纪的诗人中,如果就其代表本土而言,弗罗斯特无疑要比艾略特更具有代表性,他是一个真正意义上的代表美国移民的民族诗人,他所构筑的诗歌世界更像是一个把自然、道德观念、风土人情、对生死的态度等等融合在一起的现实,他的诗大都是从生活中的细节出发,对自然和心理的描写尤其细腻精微,如果反复阅读甚至可以从他的

There is a powerful logic of homogeneity, sinister and evil you might call, at work so that what is good poetry by a great ethnic poet might not be deemed so in an increasingly flattening world. Hence the outcome of such corruption: disintegration of traditional sensibility to pleasure and human impulse to uplifting. One last resort: Poetry begins with the imagination but is executed with the incorrigible and incorruptible means of language. No wonder poets all associate mother tongues or languages with the conception of homeland. Especially those poets, banished from their countries, scattered here and there, for whatever reason, will stick to their mother tongues as the last resort to maintain a sort of lukewarm symbolic relation with the world, even the sole raison d'être to continue to breathe till their last breath.

In sum, the trinity of poethood presents itself today in a more confusing countenance than meets the eye. Rather we might say there are myriad of manifestations of ethnicity and nationality in poetry. Countless outstanding poets in preceding generations before us have demonstrated admirably the needlessness and narrowlessness of positing a dichotomy between ethnicity/nationality and universality. A great poet is necessarily a natural foe to such Procrustean conceptions. We might readily quote the 19th century Polish poet Adam Mickiewicz whose intensely patriotic lyrics, justly ranked among the highest achievements in Polish poetry, has also endeared himself to millions of readers outside the borders of his motherland.

The superiority of writing in this vein consists in the visibility of those peculiar sensibilities and thoughts, which belong to the inner faculties of a certain race or a nation, their incomparable perfection expressed in a harmony of the union of all. To put it in another way, it is not inasmuch as they are ethnic / national poets, but inasmuch as they have availed to such an extent that they reveal an oddly welcome sensibility to pleasure, passion, natural scenery and eternal elements such as mountains, rivers, rocks, trees, flowers and grass and changeless sun, which is imputed to them as a rare faculty, the ultimate triumph of genius blossomed and achieved. Dylan Thomas strikes me as such a poet who belongs to the Wales as he does to the literary world recognized as such elsewhere.

The poetry of Robert Frost, combining pastoral imagery with solitary philosophical themes typifies 20th century America more than T. S. Eliot, the official Nobel prize winner pitted against the former, ie, the country's unofficial poet laureate. A real immigrant poet, highly lauded for his realistic depictions of rural life and his successful employment of rural settings in New England in the early twentieth century, Frost examines with facility complex

诗句中感受到美国乡土家园泥土新鲜的气息。

今天我们所强调的所谓边缘的、地域的、民族的、弱势的、少数的、女性的等等领域的写作，其实更多的是关注这些作品所表达出来的不能被替代的声音，因为有它们的存在，我们才能真正地感觉到这个世界是完整的，哪怕它们的声音还很弱小，但任何强大的力量都不应该也不能忽视它们存在的价值，不管是从社会层面还是从文化层面都应该对他们的存在和价值予以尊重，我以为持这样一种态度才会是一个文明社会不可被逾越的底线。

很多时候，诗歌的民族性、地域性与世界性在内在逻辑关系的联系上都是极为紧密的，特别是进入新世纪之后，人类在诗歌方面的翻译又进入了一个黄金时期，历史上还从来没有过这样一个诗歌被大量翻译的时代，许多诗人的作品被翻译成世界上不同的文字，最让人兴奋和感动的是不少用小语种写作的诗人，他们的作品也获得了被翻译的机会，这种现象是在以前的任何一个世纪都不曾出现过的。

一个世界性的诗歌运动，正在全世界不同的地方悄然兴起，诗歌正在回到人们的视野并进入公众生活，诗歌已经再一次成了人类和社会精神生活建设中的一部分。在物质主义和拜金主义甚嚣尘上的现实面前，诗歌又一次成了保卫人类精神家园的武器，虽然它显示的力量并没有马上被大多数人认同，但诗歌不可被替代的作用，却在人类的心灵中筑起了一道良心的高墙，当它一旦进入了人的心灵，它就能成为人类反抗一切暴力和异化的工具。

本届西昌邛海"丝绸之路"国际诗歌周的举办，就是基于这样一个宗旨和理念，我相信来自世界各地的诗人朋友，都会带着你们的智慧和信心来到这里，为构建一个更为和谐的、美满的、善意的、幸福的人类关系作出我们的贡献。不是今天才有这样的定义，只有诗人才是人类之间进行交流的最至高无上的使者！

social and moral issues, attitude towards death. Frost always tries to remain down to earth, yet behind the genial, homespun New England rustic, while "allowing both fact and intuition a bright kingdom, he speaks for many of us, he speaks better than most of us. That is to say, as a poet must." (Radcliffe Squires)

I do confess an inveterate penchant in me to always ferret out and discern the real treasures beneath the veneer of the so called marginal, local, national, weak, minority, female and give them their dues. There are truly some voices lurking somewhere, nameless, unspoken, even unspeakable. Yet their absence or presence has enriched our inner being and has made our world intact and full. Faint as they may, powers bigger than them ignore at their own perils. Due respect must be accorded them, either institutionally or culturally, a stance any civilized community shall maintain to its advantage.

In essence, the trinity ofpoethood is closely interconnected. In this new and young age of the 21st century, poetic translation has seen a surge of renaissance and revival in that more and more poems have been turned into various foreign languages around the world. What comforts me most is that some poets who compose in minority languages arrest the welcome attention of translators, a phenomenon truly unprecedented in the annals of human history.

A world wide poetry movement is in the brewing, looming on the horizon, though imperceptibly and unobtrusively. Poetry has made a comeback to our civil life . The actions of poets have contributed to the reconstruction of a new social fabric of real option of life, justice, dignity and beauty, amply represented by poetry, as antidote against infatuation with crass capitalism and the vulgarity of commercialism and materialist fetish, making way for man to find an integral way of development. Although its powers , its cohesive forces to drive changes still await better comprehension, poetry has nevertheless erected a forbidding wall in men's hearts to fend off violence, alienation and various forms of insidious social corruptions.

Once poetry descends, through poets, upon thousands upon thousands of civilians minds, "whence as from a magnet the invisible effluence is sent forth", it will bring into full play the potentials of humans, animates, and sustains the life of all. It is with this faith we host and inaugurate Xichang. Qionghai 2016 Silk Road Intl Poetry week today. We trust this sovereign gathering of poet friends, home and abroad does have the faculty to be conducive to the forging of human relationship based upon harmony, plenty, civility and happiness thanks to the liberating and unifying capacity of poetry.

一个中国诗人的非洲情结

——在2014南非姆基瓦人道主义大奖颁奖仪式上的书面致答辞

尊敬的姆基瓦人道主义基金会的各位成员,尊敬的各位朋友:

首先,我要愧疚地向各位致歉,在这样一个伟大的时刻,我不能亲自来到这个现场,来亲自见证你们如此真诚而慷慨地颁发给我的这份崇高的荣誉。我想,纵然有一千个理由,我今天没有如期站在你们中间,这无疑都是我一生中无法弥补的一个遗憾。在此,再一次请各位原谅我的冒昧和缺席。

诸位,作为一个生活在遥远东方的中国人,还在我的少年时代,我就知道非洲,就知道非洲在那个特殊的岁月里,正在开展着一场如火如荼的反殖民主义斗争,整个非洲大陆一个又一个国家开始获得民族的自由解放和国家的最后独立。这样的情景,直到今天还记忆犹新,在我们的领袖毛泽东的号召下,我们曾经走上街头和广场,一次又一次地去声援非洲人民为争取人民解放和国家独立的正义斗争。

The African Complex of A Chinese Poet
Written Speech at 2014 Mkiva Humanitarian Award Ceremony

Respected jury from Mkiva Humanitarian Foundation and distinguished members of Imbongi Yesizwe Trust, dear friends present at this grand ceremony:

First and foremost, with greatest humility I must excuse my absence in your midst today, one of the blessed recipients from afar onto this platform, to partake of a moment which speaks so eloquently of your magnanimity and generosity to confer such an honor on me. I must count this absence amongst you, which may be excused by a thousand and one reasons though, the crowning regret in my life to date and presumably I will live to the end of my days with the perennial sense of remorse gnawing at my heart. Again I beg you to accept my apology for not being able to come to speak to you in person.

Dear friends, a Chinese of Yi ethnic origin in the remote Orient, together with my generation of teenagers in the 1960's, thanks to Mao's firm diplomatic identification with third world, either ideological or cultural, I grew up taking all people of color to be my siblings. La ceur est tourjours a la gauche, so goes a French saying. Mao's high commendation of African aspirations and mounting barrage of criticism of arrogant and thoughtless Whites in the press stoked the feeling in an adolescent mind that the black continent that you inhabit was seething with an epic fight against rapacious colonists and bloody imperialists to put their scramble to rest. This passion of onslaught of us Chinese on colonialism was easily justified and magnified by almost one century of humiliations and defeats suffered at the hands of both Western and Oriental imperialists. Inspiring stories circulated that one after another African country broke loose from their former suzerainty and won independence. We now, of course, know better. The Chinese race tend to, as Prof. Vernon Mackay puts it aptly, find a vicarious joy in empathizing with African people being ascendant as a means of giving vent to the pent- up grievances against "Ocean Devils'. A vivid mental picture arises before me of how many times we youngsters, politically well attuned to the calls of our leader, took to the streets in waves of protest and demonstration of our moral support and solidarity with African brothers in their struggle for liberation and justice. It is amazing these youthful

如果不是宿命的话，我的文学写作生涯从一开始，就和黑人文学以及非洲的历史文化有着深厚的渊源。从上一个世纪六十年代相继获得独立的非洲法语国家，其法语文学早已取得了令世人瞩目的国际性声誉，尤其是20世纪30年代创办的《黑人大学生》杂志以及"黑人性"的提出，可以说从整体上影响了世界不同地域的弱势民族在精神和文化上的觉醒，作为一个来自于中国西南部山地的彝民族诗人，我就曾经把莱奥波尔德·塞达·桑戈尔和戴维·迪奥普等人视为自己在诗歌创作上的精神导师和兄长。

同样，从上一个世纪获得独立的原英国殖民地非洲国家，那里蓬勃新生的具有鲜明特质的作家文学，也深刻地影响了我的文学观和对价值的判断。尼日利亚杰出的小说家钦·阿契贝、剧作家诗人沃·索因卡，坦桑尼亚著名的斯瓦西里语作家夏巴尼·罗伯特，肯尼亚杰出的作家恩吉古，安哥拉杰出诗人维里亚托·达·克鲁兹，当然这里我还要特别提到的是，南非杰出的诗人维拉卡泽、彼得·阿伯拉罕姆斯、丹尼斯·布鲁特斯以及著名的小说家纳丁·戈迪默等等，他们富有人性并发出了正义之声的作品，让我既感受到了非洲的苦难和不幸，同时，也真切地体会到了这些划时代的作品，同样也把忍耐中的希望以及对未来的憧憬呈现在了世界的面前。我可以毫不夸张并自信地说，在中国众多的作家和诗人中，我是在精神上与遥远的非洲联系得最紧密的一位。对此，我充满着自豪。因为我对非洲的热爱，来自于我灵魂不可分割的一个部分。

memories of idealism and agitation spring to mind all the more sweeter today than yesterday, this year than last year.

As luck would have it, or I guess karma plays a role, I embarked upon my literary career with what I would call an African complex, in my unconscious, that is, an instinctive aping of African writing techniques and styles fed upon a deep love of African cultures and peoples . We know parallel to the rise of de- colonized Africa in the late 1960s there was a gratifying development of African literature, because of its admittedly great intrinsic value, it is now widely known enough to be considered one of the major bodies of world literature. I must make mention of a few French speaking giants' names, whom I have taken as mentor and model in my poetic writing, i. e. Leopold Sedar Senghor (Senegal) Aime Cesaire (Martinique) who co - founded the reviewL'etudiants Noir in 1935 and of course, David Diop who was such an unbelievable bard. The magazine formulated the revolutionary concept of Negritude which emphasized the cultural values of the Negro, Antillese folklore and the basic dignity of the Negro race. I use the word revolutionary deliberately because it has served a prise de conscience not only for the entire Negro, but by hindsight, for all the disadvantaged groups scattered across each corner of the globe like me.

I am in the debt not only of writers and poets from Francophonie countries but also to literary geniuses from British Commonwealth, as the latter has evolved a spiritual tradition equally worthy of the name which has exerted a profound influence upon my worldview and my scale of values, although they appear somewhat reticent about the concept of Negritude, an attitude perhaps born of the particular cultural and political realities that confronted them still seeking independence. This is an illustrious galaxy, say, of the wonderful novels by Chinua Achebe (Nigeria), the brilliant plays of Wole Soyinka (Nigeria), the accomplishedcontes of Swahili speaking writer Shaaban Robert who spins his yarns so deftly (Tanzania) . They have taught me, as how to retain my footing in my Yi heritage and with what fidelity to preserve a genuinely lyrical style. I must also salute Ngugi wa Thiong'o from Kenya, Viriato Clemente da Cruz from Angola, in particular, your great Benedict Wallet Vilakazi, Peter Abrahams, Denis Brutus, and last but not least, the Nobel prize winner Nadine Gordimer. Their work derives from Nero's suffering

朋友们，我从未来到过美丽的南非，但我却对南非有着持久不衰的向往和热情，我曾经无数次地梦见过她。多少年来，我一直把南非视为人类在二十世纪后半叶以来，反对种族隔离、追求自由和公正的中心。我想这并非是偶然。

我还在二十多岁的时候，就在诗歌《古老的土地》里，深情地赞颂过非洲古老的文明和在这片广袤的土地上生活着的勤劳善良的人民。当二十世纪就要结束的最后一个月，我写下了献给纳尔逊·曼德拉的长诗《回望二十世纪》，同样，当改变了二十世纪历史进程的世界性伟人，纳尔逊·曼德拉离开我们的时候，我又写下了长诗《我们的父亲》，来纪念这位人类的骄子，因为他是我们在精神上永远不会死去的父亲。是的，朋友们，从伟大的纳尔逊·曼德拉的身上，我们看到了伟大的人格和巨大的精神所产生的力量，这种力量，它会超越国界、种族以及不同的信仰，这种伟大的人格和精神，也将会在这个世界的每一个角落，深刻地影响着人类对自由、民主、平等、公正的价值体系的重构，从而为人类不同种族、族群的和平共处开辟出更广阔的道路。伟大的南非，在此，请接受我对你的敬意！

and woes the compelling pathos and distinguishable hope for a better world and gives insight into the social and political evolution of the whole continent, the trajectory per se of South Africa from an apartheid state toward a democracy . They certainly suggest a recipe of success for all indigenous writers and poets like me in our strenuous search for a vigorous and prospective writing. I might safely vaunt, among all the established and emerging Chinese writers and poets, my spiritual bond with African traditions has been unmistakably unassailable. I say this with the fullest extent of assurance and pride for the simple but ample reason that Africa has been thrice the object of my keenest attachment, emotional, intellectual and poetic.

Friends, I have never set a foot upon the soil of your beautiful land, yet this country called by the name of South Africa has been the Mecca that has titillated my Imagination for all my life. Yes, remote and distant, I have nevertheless chanced upon your country for innumerable times in dream, between midnight and dawn when sleep comes in snatches. Since the latter part of the 20th century, South Africa has been my Stalingrad to thwart and crack the segregationist walls of Apartheid, an apocalyptical war wherein human destiny hangs on a single thread of confrontation between justice and injustice, tyranny and freedom, equality and oppression. Not without a good reason.

Back in the 1980s, when a youth aspirant of the laurel crown of the Muses, I wrote a poem hailing the antiquity of African civilizations and extolling the numerous virtues of Black people. Your industry, your innocence and courage has been one of my themes. As the last month of the 20th century plodded its way towards eventuality, I dedicated a long poem Looking Back to the 20th Century to Nelson Mandela, the man who has acquired an iconic epoch-making standing in the minds of peoples across all the five known continents. Again when the most saddening news of his departure from the human scene reached me, my heart contracted with grief and pain, I penned a long poem entitled Our Father to elegize and mourn over the untimely decaying of this "icon of the times" who has had such enormous impact on the domestic and global politics of our time and remains immortal to my memory and posterity. To quote Clinton, Mandela "simply soldiered on, raging against injustice and leading us towards the light." The former American president makes a point worth emphasizing. Nelson Mandela, a born leader, afire with the faith in the

朋友们，我知道，姆基瓦人道主义大奖是为纪念南非著名的人权领袖、反对种族隔离和殖民统治的斗士理查德·姆基瓦而设立的。这个奖曾颁发给我们十分崇敬的纳尔逊·曼德拉、肯·甘普、菲德尔·卡斯特罗等政要和文化名人。我为获得这样一个奖项，而感到万分的荣幸。基金会把我作为一个在中国以及世界各地推动艺术和文化发展的领导人物，并授予我"世界性人民文化的卓越捍卫者"的称号，这无疑是对我的一种莫大的鼓励。

同样在此时此刻，我的内心也充满着一种惶恐和不安，因为我为这个世界人类多元文化的传承和保护，所做出的创造性工作和贡献还非常有限，作为中国少数民族作家学会的现任会长，作为中国在地方省区工作的一位高级官员，同时也作为一个行动的诗人，我一直在致力于多民族文化的保护和传承，并把这种传承和保护，作为一项神圣的职责。在我的努力下，青海湖国际诗歌节、青海国际诗人帐篷圆桌会议、达基沙洛国际诗人之家写作计划、诺苏艺术馆暨国际诗人写作中心对话会议、三江源国际摄影节、世界山地纪录片节、青海国际水与生命音乐之旅以及青海国际唐卡艺术与文化遗产博览会已经成为了中国进行国际文化交流和对话的重要途径和平台。尽管如此，我深知在这样一个全球化的时代，跨国资本和理性技术的挤压，人类文化多样性的生存空间，已经变得越来越狭小，从这个意义上而言，我们所有的开创性工作，也才算有了一个初步的开头。

indomitable character of human hope, lives an epic life of hardship, resilience, eventual triumph and ultimate forgiveness of his Afrikaner opponents, revealing a towering personality and a luminous spirit that transcend racial, religious and national barriers and helping shape the trend of things to come. He awakens an echo dormant in men's hearts. He drives us all to noble deeds. He senses the absolute necessity of our time in the reevaluation and restructuring of our scales of norms and values, such as freedom, justice, fairness and equality to pave way for a more humanistic and peacefully co-existent future. Dear and great South Africa, please accept our sincerest and warmest congratulations, owing to one vital fact of your best son of Nelson Mandela, you have earned my eternal admiration and I am returning to the fold, South Africa, my second spiritual home.

Friends, I am wide awake to the fact that Mkiva Humanitarian Awards were established in 1999 in honor of another Mandela like hero, Richard Mkiva, from a obscure Bolotwa village of Dutywa, a community activist and a fighter for the rights of the rural communities, now also enshrined as a symbol of resistance against the apartheid policies and laws. I am really flattered to enter this Hall of Fame with resounding celebrities like Nelson Mandela, Fidel Castro, President Rawlings and Dr Salim Ahmed Salim as gigantic predecessors. I count myself, both humbled and blessed as you, all the distinguished jury, judge me as taking initiatives and orchestrating a number of cultural events that have somewhat global repercussions and conferring upon me the glorious title of "Champion of Peoples Freedom." What a boon to my ego! What a boost for my tenuous endeavor to enhance cultural diversity and conservation of cultural heritage in a remote economic backwater province of China!

Words fail me at this moment. Uneasiness and irritation seep in. The difficulty is that I have rendered this troubled and tormented world a very small, albeit useful, service. True, for years in my office as vice governor, I deem it incumbent upon me to protect our physical and spiritual country and my efforts have borne some fruits as I have pioneered, as initiator and architect, the successful staging of several cultural events, either yearly or biannual, such as Qinghai Lake International Poetry Festival, Qinghai Tent Roundtable Forum for World Poets, Sanjiangyuan International Photographing Festival, World-Mountain Documentary Festival, Musical Tour of Qinghai International Water & Life Concert as well as Qinghai International Thangka and Cultural Heritage

为此，我将把这一崇高的来自非洲的奖励，看成是你们对伟大的中国和对勤劳、智慧、善良的中国人民的一种友好的方式和致敬，因为中国政府和中国人民，在南非人民对抗殖民主义的侵略和强权的每一个时期，都坚定地站在南非人民所从事的正义事业的一边，直至黑暗的种族隔离制度最终从这个地球上消失。

今年是南非民主化二十周年，我们知道，新南非在1994年的首次民主选举，让南非成功地避免了一场流血冲突和内战，开启了一条寻求和平协商的道路，制定了高举平等原则的南非新宪法，二十年过去了，我们今天看到的新南非，仍然是一个稳定繁荣与民主的国度。我们清楚地知道，中国和南非同属金砖国家，我们有着许多共同的利益，两国元首在互访中所确定的经济、贸易和文化上的交流任务，为我们未来的发展指明了方向，我相信，未来的中国和未来的南非都将会更加地美好。

Exhibition Fair. I have also raised money for two other cultural enterprises, i. e. a modern Yi Art Museum and a Dajishaluo International Poets House now under hot construction. Essential to my initiative is Qinghai's extreme alpine topography and remote mountainous terrain as famed Roof of the World, which supports a diversity of bio- species of irreplaceable value. No less important is the region as potpourri of multi- religions, multi- races and multi- cultures. I do dream of using art to bring to the world's attention the elemental processes of human cultures attached to the mountainous terrain, to enact dialogues between various cultures, to enhance the harmonious relationship between man and nature and assist the public to understand the implications of the environmental cataclysms that might jeopardize the alpine eco- system in the wake of the sweeping reckless modernization.

Infinitesimal as my contribution, your award comes as the highest token of recognition not only for my relentless bid of cultural import, but also as a gentle reminder of warm friendship that is evolving between Chinese people and South African people, simply because at each critical juncture for the last 70 years, our government and our people have chosen unswervingly to align with you in your heroic struggle to trample under feet the shameful Apartheid and other forms of insidious repression until the bright day of justice and e- quality emerged.

2014 marks the 20th anniversary of a new democratized South Africa, the first general election being successfully held after the most ignoble chapter in your history was turned. A bloody internecine war was evaded. Instead, a path of peaceful reconciliation and constitutional republic embracing for the first time citizens of color was blazed, pacesetting for still some to follow, awe- inspiring for many to watch breathless. The euphoria that accompanied the release of Nelson Mandela from Rueben Island has been well exploited and founded, as the past 20 years has seen the growth of a new South Africa, a land of political stability, economic prosperity and cultural brilliance. Belonging to the same bloc of the Bricks, Sino- South African relations have run smoothly due to a plethora of interests common to both sides. Presidents of both countries have exchanged visits and outlined agendas of cooperation touching the sectors of economics, cultures and trade, pointing to a promising tomorrow for both countries.

最后，请允许我表达这样一种心意，那就是再一次向姆基瓦人道主义基金会，致以我最深切的感激之情，因为你们的大胆而无私的选择，我的名字将永远与伟大的南非，与伟大的理查德·姆基瓦的名字联系在了一起。同样，我将会把你们给我带来的这样一种自豪，传递给我千千万万的同胞，我相信，他们也将会为此而感到由衷的自豪。谢谢大家！

To conclude, let me reiterate: I must convey my deepest gratitude to Mkiva Humanitarian Foundation and Imbongi Yesizwe Trust. Your daring and selfless decision to make me the recipient of your award has once and for all, welded my name with the worthier name of Richard Mkiva, with great South Africa. What is left on my part is to impart the sense of pride and elation such an accolade has sparkled in me to millions upon millions of my country folks. I assure you, this honor to me is also theirs. Thanks for your attention.

在 2016 欧洲诗歌与艺术荷马奖颁奖仪式上的致辞

尊敬的欧洲诗歌与艺术荷马奖评委会，尊敬的各位朋友，我亲爱的同胞们：

今天对于我来说，是一个喜出望外的日子，我相信对于我们这个数千年来就生活在这片高原的民族而言，也将会是一个喜讯，它会被传播得比风还快。感谢欧洲诗歌与艺术荷马奖评委会，你们的慷慨和大度体现在对获奖者全部创作和思想的深刻把握，更重要的是你们从不拘泥于创作者的某一个局部，而是把他放在了一个民族文化和精神的坐标高度，由此不难理解，你们今天对我的选择，其实就是对我们彝民族古老、悠久、灿烂而伟大的文化传统的褒奖，是馈赠给我们这片土地上耸立的群山、奔腾的河流、翠绿的森林、无边的天空以及所有生灵的一份最美好的礼物。

尤其让人不知所措、心怀不安的是，你们不远万里，竟然已经把这一如此宝贵的赠予送到了我的家门，可以说，此时此刻我就是这个世界上一个幸运的人。按照我们彝族人的习惯，在这样的时候，我本不应该站在这里，应该做的是在我的院落里为你们宰杀牲口，递上一杯杯美酒，而不是站在这里浪费诸位的时间。

朋友们，这个奖项是以伟大的古希腊诗人荷马的名字命名的，《伊利亚特》和《奥德赛》两部伟大的史诗，为我们所有的后来者都树立了光辉的榜样。当然，这位盲歌手留下的全部遗产，都早已成了人类精

Noble Literature Is Still of Interest and Moment

Acceptance Speech at the Awarding Ceremony of

The European Medal of Poetry and Art Homer 2016

Respected judges of the Chamber of The European Medal of Poetry and Art Homer 2016, Respected friends, my own Yi compatriots:

Fortune has dealt with me rather too well and I should be grateful for the breaking of another dawn as it comes in such an auspicious manner , that is, today begins with such extraordinary honours like The European Medal of Poetry and Art Homer 2016 conferred upon me. You might rest assured good tidings in this remote location of my beloved land travel like wildfire among my own tribesmen and tribeswoman. The prize has been altogether popular with both me and my people because it indicates an European perspective that noble literature is still of interest and moment as well as a recognition that my poetry , deeply rooted in the national traits of the Yi people , contains the whole of ethnic Nuosu , and as such, bears the social and aesthetic significance to a pre-eminent degree despite critical doubts of my tenacious harping on the arch theme of the Yi identity pitted against modernity as well as grudges as to the insularity of my writings from some quarters. No wonder your option of me , for me , constitutes a timely solute to the Yi spirituality, so ancient, so marvelous, so glorious rivaling any other counterpart. Your prize comes also as a most suitable gift to this land , all the sentient beings full of song and virtue , its towering peaks, its wild torrents, its perpetually forested woods, its perpetually crystal clear skies, its grassy slopes scented with nameless wild flowers.

At this moment I must sound very Unnuosu and perhaps cumbersome as to present my gratitude with a plain thank you considering you have traveled around the world to my doorstep to deliver this distinction. Why me? Well, the Yi protocols of friendship dictate, to bearers of good tidings like you, my absence amidst you in this moment, or rather , the Yi cult of generosity commands me not stand here to mouth some platitudes of courtesy, but to hurry and scurry as a helper in the courtyard to butcher a goat, a bull and a swine or as the blessed host to encourage the guests drink one more toast as befits authentic Nuosus

神文化最重要的源头之一。在这里，我不想简单地把这位智者和语言世界的祭司比喻成真理的化身，而是想在这里把我对他的热爱用更朴素的语言讲出。在《伊利亚特》中，阿基琉斯曾预言他的诗歌将会一直延续下去，永不凋零。对这样一个预言我不认为是一种宿命式的判断，其实直到今天，荷马点燃的精神火焰就从未有过熄灭。

然而最让我吃惊和感动的是，如果没有荷马神一般的说唱，那个曾经出现过的英雄时代，就不会穿越时间，哪怕它就是青铜和巨石也会被磨灭，正是因为这位神授一般的盲人，让古希腊的英雄谱系，直到现在还活在世上熠熠生辉。

讲到这里，朋友们，你们认为这个世界所发生的一切，都是由偶然的因素构成的吗？显然不是，正如我今天接受这样一个奖项，在这里说到伟大的荷马，似乎都在从空气和阳光中接受一个来自远方的讯息和暗示，那就是通过荷马的神谕和感召，我再一次重新注视和回望我们彝民族伟大的史诗《勒俄》《梅葛》以及《阿细的先基》；再一次屹立在自然和精神的高地，去接受太阳神的洗礼；再一次回到我们出发时的地方。作为一个在这片广袤的群山之上有着英雄谱系的诗人，原谅我在这里断言：因为我的民族，我的诗不会死亡！谢谢诸位！卡沙沙！

at the feast.

Dear Friends, this medal to me is named after Homer, the supreme poet of the ancient Occidental world. And with Homer, the two great epics of Iliad and Odyssey, the oldest extant works of the West, have now been an essential part of literature, West and East, a veritable legacy left to posterity by this blind poet deemed the twin fountainheads of Western cultural tradition. At this point I hesitate to compare Homer, the prophet and the Brahman of poetry to the incarnation of truth. He certainly is. And much more. I really would like to tell, in unguarded frankness, unabashed sincerity, my growing admiration for his merits over time. Simplicity, unadorned language and being true to life are some of Homer's reputed qualities. There is a nobility and dignity to his simple and direct lines. In Iliad, Achilles foretells his poems will endure and will never burn to a cinder. To such prophecy, my assent is total and until this day, can't you see the literary sky is still ablaze with Homerian songs and hymns?

What perennially holds me in awe is the fact, without a blind trabadour in the 8th century BC, our literary history would have been much deprived and depopulated. The calling of the roll of heroes like Achilles and Agamemnon, though boisterous and frivolous, has always dignified and enlivened even as bronze will rust and boulders will decompose.

Mind you, my friends, I speak of this award with pride, one associated with the great Homer. It seems like a stroke of telepathy, a mysterious message or oracle from Homer, and affected by the powers of such an oracle, I turn my gaze, to all intents and purposes, again at the Yi epics, Leer, Meige as well as Aji's Xianji. all being splendid glorification of everything in the Daliangshan Highland. Entranced, I seem to have ascended again the majestic heights of Nature and Spirituality of this beloved Yi land ready for the sacred baptism of the Sun God. Literally and literarily, I am back to where I embarked upon my virgin journey into the outside world 30 odd years ago. Allow my egoism, a poet inheriting such an illustrious genealogy of heroes as Homer sings hymns to, I rejoice at this moment, with my dear Nuosu folks, by virtue of being the Nuosu bard associated with the right of prophecy, that my poems will last and continue to shine before the world thanks to my people, because of them and for the sake of them. Thank you for your attention. Kasasa!

THE EUROPEAN MEDAL OF POETRY AND ART

Homer 2016

Jidi Majia - China

Laudation

Jidi Majia is one of the greatest contemporary Chinese poets. His poetry is culturally bounded, which is in fact deeply rooted to the tradition of the nation, Nuosu. He also wrote poetry to enhance the ancient magical consciousness that is moderated by priests Bimo holding the spirits of his ancestors. Form of his art is an invisible space of spirituality, from which mountain people remain in constant interaction, that clarifies to bestow the age of great human longing for purity and fulfilment. Living in the face of vastness and natural beauty, his work constantly strives to reflect the depth of human fate, over which it slopes, and connects to the large cosmogonic systems and the elementary mechanisms of duration. It has sensed eternity through completion of day and night; sticking to the human body, with its illness and pain, its vigils in the shape of a human, exposes to weather conditions, that is subjected to be the destructive power of time. It is rare and appears to be so clear to human consciousness, shimmering to ever shape a bright beam, penetrating to the large time intervals, and scanning space in all its shapes and metamorphoses. Majia can write a poem similar to the gentle movement of the wings of dragonflies, and create wide panoramas, which reflects the spirit of a whole epoch, the ethos of free existence in the midst of mountains and lakes, in harmony with animals, birds and all living beings. Every scene of his poem becomes the continuation of the story of the tribe, as if it is specially appointed to proclaim its glory. The poet is aware that his work has been selected from the many in order to fulfill his desired destiny. He understood that he could not live permanently in the mountains of Liangshan, where he could go out with a shotgun for hunting and lead a peaceful life only with his family clan. He could dance around campfires and look into the distance from the top of the mountain, but his virtue is set to be among the poets of the world, and proclaim the glory of his land and people in the farthest corners of the globe. He could sing in small huts, separated from the cold, cosmic distance, he could listen to the stories of

2016年欧洲诗歌与艺术荷马奖颁奖词

吉狄马加是中国最伟大的当代诗人之一，他的诗富有文化内涵，事实上深深植根于彝族的传统。他的诗歌创作也提升了通灵祖先的毕摩祭司所把控的远古魔幻意识。他的诗歌艺术构成一片无形的精神空间，山民们与这一空间保持持久的互动，他的诗让人心灵净化，并构建起一个人类不懈追求纯真和自我实现的伟大时代。面朝广袤美丽的自然，他的作品始终致力于表现人类命运的深度，这命运的陡坡一直通向宏大的宇宙体系和存在的基本机制。这一切借助昼夜的更替被永恒地感知；这一切化身为守夜人，躯体遭受打击，忍受疾病和痛苦，他面对风霜雪雨，承受着时间的毁灭力量。人类的意识得到如此清晰地呈现，它甚至构成一道闪亮的光束，穿透巨大的时间间隔，扫描各种形状、各类变体的空间，这对于诗歌而言十分罕见。吉狄马加能像蝴蝶翅膀轻盈扇动那般写出一首诗，他也能创作出视野宽广的全景图，这些全景图反映整个时代的精神，也反映人类在山川湖畔与鸟兽等一切生物和谐共处的自由存在特质。他诗中的每一抒情场景均成为一则部落故事之延续，似在特意宣示他的部落之荣光。诗人意识到，他的作品脱颖而出，正是为了完成他渴望的使命。他深知，他无法继续定居凉山，背着猎枪去打猎，在族人中间过着悠闲、宁静的生活。他本可围着篝火舞蹈，站在山巅远眺，可他的命运却是跻身于世界诗人之列，宣示他那偏居地球一隅的故土和人

elders and shamans, but his work interpretes the elementary truth of existence: I am a Nuosu! This is his great task, and at the same time a kind of prayer that is repeated for generations, in a series of reminders and sublimations, a distant echo of history that reflects the past and the glorious future.

民之荣光；他本可在小茅屋里歌唱，远离寒冷的宇宙，聆听长辈和巫师讲故事，可他的工作却是一遍又一遍地重申存在的基本真理："我是彝人！"这是他的伟大任务，同时也是世代传诵的祈祷，借助一连串的提示和升华，这也是能反映过去、亦能再现壮丽未来的历史所发出的遥远回声。

此篇颁奖词的中文译者为刘文飞。

诗歌译者

梅丹理，美国诗人，中英文翻译者，俄亥俄州立大学中文硕士。曾担任美国宾州大学东亚语文系讲师，现任北京中坤基金翻译顾问、台湾日月潭涵静书院研究员。译作包括冯友兰的《三松堂全集自序》（夏威夷大学出版社）、真华法师的《参学琐谭》（纽约州立大学出版社）、朱朱的《一幅画的诞生》（湖南美术出版社）。诗歌翻译包括《麦城诗选》（*Selected Poems of Mai Cheng*, Shearsman Books, 2009）；奚密、马悦然编的《台湾新诗选》（*Frontier Taiwan*, 哥伦比亚大学出版社, 2005）；杨四平编的《当代中文诗歌选》（*Contemporary Chinese Poetry*, 上海文艺出版社, 2007）；吉狄马加的《黑色狂欢曲》（*Rhapsody in Black*, 俄克拉荷马大学出版社, 2014）、骆英的《文革记忆》（*Memories of the Cultural Revolution*, 俄克拉荷马大学出版社, 2015）。他翻译的当代诗人还包括严力、阎志、杨克。其个人英文诗集 *Man Cut in Wood* 于 2004 年由洛杉矶 Valley Contemporary Poets 出版。

Denis Mair holds an M. A. in Chinese from Ohio State University and has taught at University of Pennsylvania. He is currently a research fellow at Hanching Academy, Sun Moon Lake, Taiwan. He translated autobiographies by the philosopher Feng Youlan (Hawaii University Press) and the Buddhist monk Shih Chen-hua (SUNY Press). His translation of art criticism by Zhu Zhu was published by Hunan Fine Arts Press (2009). He has translated poetry by Yan Li, Mai Cheng, Meng Lang, Luo Ying, Jidi Majia, and many others. He also translated essays by design critic Tang Keyang and art historian Lü Peng for exhibitions they curated respectively in 2009 and 2011 at the Venice Biennial. (See Lü Peng, From San Servolo to Amalfi, Charta Books, Milan, 2011).

文章译者

黄少政,1958年出生。1982年毕业上海外语学院。2011年重译纪伯伦,提出复译伦理,出版译作《先知·沙与沫》(漓江出版社);2012年出版《翻译的成色》(广西师范大学出版社);2013年,承担外研社吉狄马加文学文化演讲翻译;2015年复译《圣经新约》(台湾思行文化出版公司)。

Huang Shaozheng, who translated Jidimajia's literary and cultural speeches of this volume, is an independent translation scholar and translator based in Qinghai Normal University with two monographs and five translations to his credit. Major works include *Translation Or Creation?* (2004), *Translation Paid In Gold* (2012), *Prophet by Gibran-A new Translation* (2012), *In the Name of Land and Life-Jidimajia's Literary and Cultural Speeches* (2013), *New Testament* (2015).

图书在版编目（ＣＩＰ）数据

从雪豹到马雅可夫斯基：汉英对照 / 吉狄马加著；梅丹理，黄少政译. -- 武汉：长江文艺出版社, 2016.11
ISBN 978-7-5354-8903-6

Ⅰ. ①从… Ⅱ. ①吉… ②梅… ③黄… Ⅲ. ①诗集－中国－当代－汉、英 Ⅳ. ①I227

中国版本图书馆CIP数据核字(2016)第 149703 号

策　　划：沉　河	
责任编辑：谈　骁	责任校对：陈　琪
封面设计：尚书堂•叫兽	责任印制：左　怡　邱　莉

出版：长江出版传媒　长江文艺出版社
地址：武汉市雄楚大街 268 号　　邮编：430070
发行：长江文艺出版社
电话：027—87679360
http://www.cjlap.com
印刷：荆州市翔羚印刷有限公司

开本：640 毫米×970 毫米　　1/16　　印张：19.5　插页：6 页
版次：2016 年 11 月第 1 版　　　　　　2016 年 11 月第 1 次印刷
行数：8181 行

定价：39.00 元

版权所有，盗版必究（举报电话：027—87679308　　87679310）
（图书出现印装问题，本社负责调换）